JACK IN THE BOX
A Jack of All Trades novel

DH Smith

Earlham Books

Published 2016 by Earlham Books
Book design & cover art by Lia at Free Your Words
(*www.FreeYourWords.com*)

ISBN: 978-1-909804-23-4

THE CAST & SETTING

1

STARGAZING

57

UP ON THE ROOF

95

PRISONERS

145

PART ONE:
THE CAST & SETTING

Chapter 1

It would be a good job to get mid month, close to home. Jack could walk there in ten minutes, but you never could be sure what tools you might need on a job, so best drive. Forget a drill, a saw, a club hammer – and he'd end up coming back to get them. So he was driving over the road humps of Earlham Grove in Forest Gate. Poor and well-off side by side. Many of the big Victorian houses were broken up into flats, some into separately let rooms, seriously overcrowded.

He bumped over a sleeping policeman, the sun shining on all and sundry. A Muslim woman was walking slowly on the pavement in a black burqa, covered from head to foot, just a free strip for her eyes, where she had glasses, a concession to modernity.

Hard not to harbour some prejudice. One judged against the norms of youth. But he'd had to unlearn, as in his work he walked into varied rooms. A builder has to be nice to people if he wants to be paid and recommended. He shouldn't judge, but he did in a flick, all the time. The unknown woman was behind him. He'd never recognise her again. And that was perhaps the point.

He stopped at Woodgrange Road, the local high street. Four betting offices, he couldn't keep up with the number of fried chicken shops, a small Tesco, two bakers, a Co-op supermarket and a surprising number of internet cafes that came and went but never sold a cup of tea. A break in the traffic, and he was across, turning right on to the high street. Then past the shoebox of a church hall and the church itself where twenty feet up in the air, a thin man, seemingly attached only by his feet, harangued the crowds, pointing to the book in his right hand. But the crowds walked past heedless, no doubt making him angrier for their imperilled souls.

Jack took a left into Claremont Road, one of several roads named after royal houses, the others Windsor, Hampton, Osborne, Balmoral and Richmond, constituting the wealthiest part of the London borough of Newham, though not everyone who lived on the royal roads considered themselves rich. A relative term, depending on who was doing the counting. Some who lived here had been lucky, buying on a dip in the housing cycle. Now they had an asset worth, or at least someone was prepared to pay, one million with some properties on the verge of two. In Newham!

The royal roads made up the Woodgrange Estate, a conservation area. Owners had to conserve the Victorian appearance. Fair enough, he thought, you came to live here because you liked the area – so keep it up. It's not a free for all.

For himself, he had the basics, a roof over his head. Two rooms, a kitchen, a bathroom and a mortgage which he was hard pressed to keep paying. Local jobs were a bonus. Plenty of time for breakfast, no travel time or fares. And with the mortgage pressing, the wolf licked his lips when he saw Jack leave home.

Past Forest Gate Point, a twelve storey tower block with many of its flats sold off, and rented back to the Council at three times the price. And into the double frontages of houses in the conservation area. He drove slowly, looking at the door numbers. There was the house. Yellow brick, two storeys with Victorian embellishments of classical plasterwork round the windows and floral columns at the door. The curtains were closed on the front windows, but through the left-hand bay window he could see a glimmer of light. The house was supposed to be empty. Maybe someone else was working there. He'd park up and find out.

There were cars along the kerb on both sides, but he found a gap not too far away and walked back. The road intimidated him: up-market cars, people carriers, BMWs, the odd Mercedes, and the tip-top condition of the houses. Though just opposite was a rundown house, probably an old lady on her own, with four smelly cats, who could easily raise money on the house itself for general repairs and decorations, to be paid when she died, but why bother? If the front room leaked, then close it up and move along the hallway, and when that leaked – close that one and move to the interior.

Jack stood at the gate of the house and pondered. He was in overalls but just had a notebook and tape with him as he was only here to do an estimate. That light downstairs. He could ring the bell but he'd been told to get the key from next door. Always best to do what you're told. This job would be so convenient, but who knows how many estimates they were getting. Though if he did get it, did a good job, perhaps they'd pass his name on and he'd be the conservation area's favourite builder, his van, *Jack of All Trades,* his roving ad, here and there, on these posh streets.

He went next door to get the key.

The house was similar, two stories, fake columns at the door and windows. Brick temples. A silver grey Porsche in the drive, shaved grass in the centre and round the edges neatly pruned rose bushes just sprouting into leaf. He took the few stairs in one stride, and stood at the door. There was a single bell. No multiple occupancy this end. He rang.

The sun came from behind a cloud, as the door opened, to reveal a youngish woman, dark brown hair to her shoulders, tall, slim, no make up, in black jeans and T-shirt. He tried hard not to ogle, this was business, though you never knew.

'Hello,' she said through immaculate teeth, testimony to good parenting or expensive dentistry.

3

'Builder for next door,' he said.

She peered down the road, evidently spotting his van. 'Jack of All Trades.' She smiled. 'I'm Jan. I've been expecting you. Jack is it?' He nodded. She thought for a second, passing a hand through her hair. 'You'd best come in.'

She turned and he saw she was barefooted. He felt clumsy in his boots on the thick cream carpet, and stomped them vigorously on the mat before following her. He passed a large room which was well lit in a whitish light with various drawings laid out on the floor. Then he was past, curiosity roused. Something arty.

Jan turned into a large kitchen, high, dark wood cupboards all round, and the usual white goods. An eating area was made up of a thick wall of rough brick with a sea-green marble slab for a top. She picked up a half-filled coffee pot.

'Coffee?'

He hesitated. 'I probably should get started.'

'Have a coffee,' she said. 'There's complications.'

Her double invitation was enough, making it clear he wasn't skiving. 'Then I will. Smells good. Better than the instant I make.'

'I live on coffee,' said Jan. 'Keeps me awake and nervy. I'm probably hooked, but I don't mug pensioners, just get on with my work.'

Jack perched on a high stool. She took one herself as she poured coffee into two mugs.

'What do you do?' he said, 'if you don't mind me asking?'

She smiled, a gleaming smile, as she passed Jack a coffee. 'Do you know *Mimi the Space Cat*? I won't be offended if you don't.'

He flicked his fingers in recognition. 'I do actually,' he said. 'I used to read them to my daughter. There's the cat, Mimi, Jake the spaceman and that miserable computer, and a robot whose name I've forgotten...'

'Obo,' she said. 'I write and illustrate them. Done fifteen. They do quite well. Though to tell the truth, I am getting fed up with them. And running out of story lines.' She waved her empty hands as if to show there was no inspiration there.

'Well, my daughter liked them,' he said, 'and even my ex, she's a teacher, found them acceptable. She'd throw away anything that she thought wasn't.'

'I can see why she's your ex.'

They smiled at each other and Jack wondered whether she had another half. Her pale hands surrounded her mug, the nails very pink, the cuticles revealed like setting moons. As she drank, he thought, she's not rushing me out, either she's out of ideas, or looking for new ones.

Concentrate, he reprimanded himself as he poured milk in his coffee.

'So what's the problem next door?'

'Squatters,' said Jan.

'Right,' he said thoughtfully. 'Empty houses, always a temptation, especially round here. Do you know the landlord?'

'I don't,' she said. 'I just get emails from Terry. I don't know whether Terry is a man or a woman. I assume a woman.'

He chuckled. 'I thought he was a bloke.'

She shrugged. 'Never seen her. I've only lived here a few months. Well anyway, Terry first contacted me by email. I don't know how she got it or knew I lived next door, but that doesn't really matter... And she offered me £200 a month to hold the keys and keep an eye on things.' She half smiled. 'I don't need the money but I work from home, so it's no chore. Vastly overpaid for very little. She asked me a few days ago if I knew a local builder and I'd seen your van running around, so I looked up your website...'

'My daughter did it. She's 12.'

'It is pretty amateurish,' Jan said, 'but I figured you were a builder not a web designer.'

'And can't afford a pukka one,' he said, a little hurt and trying not to show it.

She pursed her lips. 'False economy.'

That irritated him. Another one of these well-heeled women telling him how to spend money he hadn't got. Just like Alison.

'Well, thanks for recommending me,' he said, 'in spite of the crap website.'

'Well, it's muddled, if you don't mind me saying,' she said, 'and if I wasn't so busy...'

He thought of reminding her that she wasn't so busy at this very moment, chatting with a stray builder, but then she'd got him the job. Well, not a job as yet.

'Are there any other builders involved?' he said.

'No,' Jan said sucking her lower lip. 'Your website has a childish amateurism, I wanted to see who'd done it.'

'So it worked,' he said. He was going off this lady fast. She'd found a weakness and was sticking her neat sharp nails in it and twisting.

'Well,' she said with a shrug, 'you call yourself *Jack of All Trades* and give yourself a website that proves it.'

It was one of those moments. Either grin and bear it or say what he thought. The former was less costly, he'd learnt from Alcohol Halt. Count ten. Drink coffee.

'If you give me the keys, Jan, I'll go next door – and we can both get on with our work,' he said.

'And now I've hurt you,' she said, her face slipping into sympathy. 'I'm tactless when it comes to art. It's my job, you see.'

'You put the boot in before I've even banged in a nail.'

'I'll do your website,' she said.

'I don't want you to do my website.'

'Get me some pictures of work you've done.'

6

'I don't want you to do my website.'

They stared at each other, catching each other's short breath. Classic standoff. He would not be belittled, but must be polite if he wanted to keep the work. All he wanted to do was get out of here. Breathe outside air.

'If you'll just give me the key to next door...' he said.

Jan's fingers went to her lips. She was hellishly attractive but so catty. He doubted she had another half, though if so, he was more than welcome to her.

'I think they've changed the locks,' she said.

'Oh, that's great!' he spat. The job was disappearing fast. He'd been belittled by Mimi the Space Cat's illustrator, and all for nothing if the squatters wouldn't let him in. 'How many are there?'

'Two men and a woman,' she said. 'I think.'

'Does Terry know he's been squatted?'

'Yes, she does.'

'What's he doing about it?'

'I don't know.'

Jack thought for a moment. All the squatters had to do was not let him in and that was that. No work, just an estimate. He finished the coffee. She was watching him intently. He caught her eye and they stared at each other, need shifting and searching like shapeless oil globules.

'My bathroom tap is leaking,' she said. 'If you've time. The back door keeps sticking.'

'I'll think about your offer on the website. It has been remarked on,' he conceded. He rose. 'I'll go next door and see if I can get in. Then come back here and see to your jobs.'

Chapter 2

Jack stood between the houses, resting on the garden wall of the one he should be visiting. He was reluctant to face the squatters. That wasn't his job. He was a builder for heaven's sake, not here to sort out ownership. And as for that woman, Jan, who did she think she was? People who live in these big houses think they own the world. So OK, he'd have to improve his website but professional people charge professional fees and first there was the mortgage to earn. Website was well down the list. Or had been.

The sort of hassle that had driven him to the world's favoured narcotic. There were at least half a dozen places on the high street he could buy the white, brown, green, or colourless liquid. Then drown the dogs of criticism. Become a baby with a baby's senses and a baby's responsibility. He reacted badly to criticism. It chewed him up. Avoid stress, said Alcohol Halt. How? It was everywhere. It was people. Walking the streets, behind every door. He'd come out of one house where a woman had had a go at him and here was another door with God knows who behind it. Building work was the easy bit. Dealing with people, the problem.

Across the road, a magnolia was coming into bloom, its whitish pink flowers beginning to pop in the warmish sun. The sky was almost clear, a good night to get the telescope out. That always soothed him, put his petty gripes into perspective, gazing into the infinite. He'd go to Alcohol Halt this evening. He needed a recharge. Meet others with the same demon. The sessions could be boring, repetitious, the regulars saying the same things over and over. Weren't drunks and ex drunks the most boring people in the world?

Himself included. Trying to claim special provision for a mundane addiction.

After he'd done his penance, he'd look at the stars, who didn't love you or hate you or determine what you were going to be or do tomorrow, but were absolutely indifferent, in the coldness of deep space.

His phone shuddered on his hip. He took it out and looked at the screen and hesitated. Alison, his ex. What was it this time? He could ignore the call, but then get kicked for that too. Besides, answering it delayed dealing with the squatters.

'Hello,' he said.

'Hello, Jack.'

It didn't sound like her telling-off voice. But then she never called for a chat. Not ever.

'I'm working now,' he half lied. 'So what can I do for you?'

'I'm looking at a house tonight,' she said, 'so can Mia stay at your place?'

He mentally adjusted. Scrap Alcohol Halt. But then Mia was better, there was no risk he'd drink with her around.

'Yes, fine,' he said.

'Good,' said Alison. 'Has she got clean clothes for school tomorrow?'

'Yes,' he lied again. Mia could wear the same clothes for two days without anyone noticing. He should get a washing machine. After he'd paid the mortgage, after he did a new website...

'The house is in your area,' she said. 'Sebert Road. Do you know it?'

'I do. Runs on to the cemetery. Only half a mile from where I am now. The Conservation Area.'

'Out of my league,' she said.

'Even now you're a Head?'

'I tell you, Jack, the money's not worth the stress. I don't know why I ever left Brighton.'

Ambition, he thought, but did not say.

'I'll be home early anyway,' he said. 'Just doing an estimate here. But Mia has a key if I'm a bit late.'

'Make sure she does her homework. Don't just go out stargazing, Jack.'

'Yes, yes... Must get back to work. Best of luck with the house hunting.'

With final goodbyes he closed the call. No telling off, but he always felt rasped with sandpaper after Alison called. Anyway, tonight was settled. He'd better do some food shopping. He always ate better when Mia came, feeling obligated to feed her properly. They got on well, mostly. She was just pre-teenage, trouble coming no doubt. But not quite yet.

So Alison was looking at a house round here. Was that good or bad news? Mixed. They were parents together, and when she was living down in Brighton that was a real chore. All that driving backwards and forwards. But Alison up the road, he wasn't sure he liked that, though Mia would be close too, drop in close, and that was fine.

And now the squatters. Evaded long enough. The worst that could happen was that they wouldn't let him in, and this job would be down the chute. He took a deep breath and turned to face the house.

The grass needed a cut, cheerful daffodils waved on either side of the tiled path. The small red and black squares were in good repair, he noted. There was double-pillared plasterwork on either side of the high-arched door. The entablatures of the pillars had a sort of floral surround, picked up in the blue and yellow flowers on the leaden glass windows. It was all the touches that made this house classy, and made him nervous. High standard repairs would be expected.

Jack was about to ring the bell when a young woman

wearing a hijab came out of next door and passed along the wall. He called to her.

'Excuse me, Miss. Anyone living here?'

She stopped by the gate. 'Some squatters,' she said. 'No trouble. As yet.'

'Do you know Terry?' he said.

'Terry?' She screwed up her face.

'The owner,' he said.

She shook her head. 'A family used to live there. From Sri Lanka. They moved last year – and we waited for someone to move in. When no one did, we wondered what was happening. Friends of our family are interested. Do you know the owner?'

'I just got an email to do some repairs,' he said. 'I'm a builder.'

'So that's your van outside our house. Jack of All Trades. I wondered who that was.'

'I'm Jack,' he said. 'I was contacted by Terry, told to get the keys from next door, the other side to you.'

'That woman on her own,' she said. 'She hasn't lived here long.' Then added quietly as if she might be overheard, 'She goes out with these big folders. What does she do?'

'She does children's books. Do you know *Mimi the Space Cat*?'

'I do. I'm a teaching assistant at Woodgrange Infants. I've read some of the stories to the kids. They love them. So she's the writer?'

'And illustrator.'

'Jan...something or other,' she flicked her fingers. 'Fletcher. That's it, Fletcher. Fancy that. We must invite her into school. A local author. Well, well.' She sucked her lower lip. 'Do you do paving?'

'I've laid plenty of paving stones,' he said confidently. Too many, he thought. Back breakers.

'Our patio needs repairing,' she said.

'My card,' said Jack, sorting one out of his wallet.

The woman took it and looked at it. 'Can't promise anything, but I'll show it to my dad. It's his house, and Mum's. I'm Amina.'

'Pleased to meet you, Amina,' he said. 'And I'd be happy to do some paving work. I only live ten minutes away. On Earlham Grove.'

'Oh, I know that. The other side of Woodgrange. Where the mail sorting office is.' She looked at her watch. 'Must go, or I'll be late for school.' She gave Jack a pleasant smile and a wave. 'Bye.'

'Bye.'

He watched her go, walking swiftly down the road. A Muslim obviously, probably born here. No accent. And a definite improvement on the sharpness of Jan Fletcher, author and illustrator of *Mimi the Space Cat* beloved by the children of Woodgrange Infants. Interestingly, Amina didn't know Terry. Neither did Jan know him/her, the supposed owner of this house. But Terry had contacted Jack, paid Jan her £200 a month, gave her a key, which was now useless as the squatters had changed the locks. It was all quite a muddle.

He'd have to watch it. And make sure he got half the money before he started work, if he got the job. He'd been stung a few times; this was one that said – cash first.

Jack rang the bell.

A loud bing-bong sang through the house, louder because of the emptiness. Whoever was in there couldn't have failed to hear it. He looked at his watch. 8.44 am. If they're not working they could still be in bed. He rang again.

If they didn't open up then that was that. He might as well go home and have breakfast. Oh yes, there was Jan next door with her leaky tap. Five minutes, what could he charge for that? If she made him breakfast, he'd do it for nothing though he shouldn't. He was a lousy capitalist. With a lousy website.

There was movement inside. A door closing, footsteps, a form in the glass of the door. It opened to reveal a young woman, bleary-eyed as if she'd just woken. She was slim and small, her feet bare and dirty. Her hair was brown with a touch of red, tousled, thick and very curly. Her blue jeans were torn at the knee and calf, one half leg it seemed hanging by a thread. She wore a check, un-ironed shirt, too big for her.

'Yes?' she said warily, rubbing one of her eyes with the back of a hand. 'What do you want?'

'I'm a builder,' he said, a foot on the top step and one lower. The notebook was in the pocket of his overalls so he'd look less officious. 'The owner sent me to do an estimate for repair work that needs doing here.'

'Nothing needs doing here,' she said firmly.

'You've got a leaky roof up there,' he pointed out a shifted tile. 'And I suspect quite a few other things. Empty houses deteriorate.'

'Entropy,' she said.

'What?' he exclaimed in surprise. A word he knew from reading about the heat death of the Universe was being applied to a house. More or less catching on, he added, 'Keeps me in work. Nothing fixes itself.'

'We're squatting,' she said emphatically. Her face was thin, expressive and quite smudged. He guessed they could do with a broom for all the dust in the house.

'I don't care who lives here,' he said. 'That's nothing to do with me. I've just been asked to do an estimate for repairs.'

'For someone who can afford to leave this house empty,' she said accusingly.

'I don't know anything about that.'

'The owner must have another house, at least one other,' she said reproachfully. 'Who knows how many he's got?'

'No idea,' said Jack, working to placate this angry woman. 'You can stay as long as you like as far as I'm concerned. I don't like to see empty houses. But look, I've a living to make.' He appealed with open hands. 'I need to get inside to do an estimate so I can get this job to pay my rent.' Rent, he deliberately said, as he thought his mortgage would anger her, making him one of the parasitic property owning class.

'You're a working man doing his job,' she said.

'I am,' he admitted. 'I don't like to work for capitalists, but what choice do you have? That's the system. They've got the money.'

'Too right.' Her lips pursed tight. 'It's not fair we should be depriving you of work,' she added thoughtfully. 'You're just an exploited member of the working class.' She pulled her ear, then added, 'I've got to talk to the others. Stay here. I'll have to close the door on you. Sorry.'

'I'll wait,' said Jack.

She nodded with a half smile, and closed the door.

Jack blew his cheeks out. That was hard work, but he was impressed at how well he'd sold himself. Agree with the customer, wasn't that the mantra? Except to a fair extent he agreed with her. Not so aggressively, but knew well enough that the rich had the best cards and did all they could to keep others from getting hold of them.

She'd made him a socialist this morning – and it wasn't yet 9 o'clock. How far left could he go by bedtime?

Inside he could hear yelling; a door must be open in the hallway. Two or was it three voices? Hers he could recognise, the others, yes it was two, were both male. Presumably her job had been to get rid of him, not to side with a downtrodden worker. He couldn't make out the words but there was a fierce scrap going on. He could half guess its content. She defending him as a worker, they attacking him as a capitalist flunky, a mere tool of the landlord.

The shouting softened. Then started up again. He had challenged their politics. They should thank him for putting them on the spot and having to get their books out. Who did anarchists read? In fact, he hardly knew what anarchists were. Not communists, he knew enough not to call them that. They didn't like leaders. Lots of meetings, lots of talking, shouting too, he could hear it. Property is theft – didn't someone say that? No one owned anything in the beginning. So how did we get to streets like this? He was doing it himself, like a guy ranting in a pub. Remaking the world.

When all he wanted was work.

If he didn't get this, then what was there? Jan the Space Cat said she'd do his website. But any work it brought in wouldn't be immediate. He could get his leaflet reprinted, stuff them through letter boxes and hope they'd gather something in. He could phone his mate Bob. He often pushed small jobs Jack's way or from time to time took him on if he needed a carpenter, Jack's main skill.

But if he couldn't even do an estimate, he certainly wouldn't get this job.

There were footsteps, a shadow on the door glass. He stood up, straightened himself. The door opened. It was the young woman, her hair half brushed.

'Sorry about that,' she said with a smile. 'The guys want to talk to you. Would you like to come in?'

'Right.' He stepped through the door and closed it behind him. He would need to be on best anarchist behaviour for the grilling. All just to do an estimate which might not get him the work anyway.

The thick hall carpet was grubby with footprints. The side walls piled with cardboard boxes, some with books in, others with papers, leaflets and posters. Did they print stuff here or just warehouse it?

As if he'd spoken, she said, 'We've an offset litho printer out the back.'

Quite a cell, he thought.

She led him into the front room. A large, long room, going from front to back of the house, like Jan's next door, with mouldings on the ceiling, around the edge, ornate in the corners and a circular floral wreath in the centre. There was no furniture. Bed rolls were on the floor, laid out on bare floorboards, the three sleeping bags like curled larvae. Clothing was scattered around, several rucksacks, shoes, an ashtray full of dog-ends and cardboard bits. There was a smell of sweat, dust and tobacco. Evidently they weren't keen on opening windows. Two young men were sitting on their sleeping bags on the floor, spooning what looked like muesli. Both were grubbily dressed, one had black print ink on his hands.

'Got trouble with your plumbing?' said Jack.

'The hot water isn't working,' said one in a very BBC accent. He was blond and blue-eyed, hair short but untidy, probably a home cut. He had long thin legs, the blue jeans sound but grubby, his red socks had holes at the toes and heels. 'We've tried but it simply won't respond.'

'You need a builder,' said Jack.

'But not a clown.' This from the other man. He was short and wiry, his teeth chipped, dark brown hair reaching his shoulders, the ends jagged.

'He's only stating the obvious, Anton,' said BBC.

'And that's why he's a clown,' said Anton glaring at Jack, his accent London, possibly local. His face was thin, eyes deep-set. He spooned his muesli with long thin fingers black with ink. 'He works for the landlord. I know his sort. Yes sir, no sir, three bags full, sir.' He turned to Jack. 'You got any principles left, mister?'

'Yes,' said Jack. He was standing at the door, not knowing how long he'd be staying.

'Like what?'

Jack looked round at the threesome. BBC and the woman were watching him, not unsympathetically, Anton apparently concentrating on his muesli, not deigning to look at a capitalist running dog.

'Like what?' he repeated.

'I don't insult people I haven't met before,' said Jack.

'Stuff your head up your bum,' exclaimed Anton, finishing his cereal.

'He's a worker,' insisted BBC. 'We don't have to be rude to him.'

'He works for the landlord class!' spluttered Anton. He put the muesli onto the floor. 'The small builder – bastion of the bourgeoisie!'

'Don't start again, Anton,' said the woman wearily. 'You said you'd hear him out.'

'I was outvoted by two revisionists,' he said grumpily. 'Listen, I know the type. You think because he's wearing overalls he's some sort of revolutionary activist? Read your Tressell.'

'Is this just a family argument, or do I get a say?' said Jack carefully.

'I know your weasel words,' spat Anton. 'Excuses. Reasons for not being part of the struggle.'

Jack had stayed leaning against the doorpost. He hadn't been invited in as he wasn't one of them. Moving from his position would be a too-obvious settling in. Anton was probably a lost cause but there were the others, and it seemed they voted on matters. How bourgeois was that.

'Anton's always like this,' said the woman to Jack with a half smile. 'I'm Susie.'

'I'm Tosh,' said BBC. Jack wondered what his real name was, having already labelled him a public school renegade.

'Jack,' he said.

'*Of All Trades*!' sneered Anton. 'I've seen your van, running up and down these streets like a whore at a sales convention.'

'Leave off,' said Tosh. 'He's a worker.'

'He's a small scale capitalist!' yelled Anton, 'dreaming of being Taylor Woodrow!'

Jack laughed, holding his belly. The very idea of being in that league was outrageous.

'My dream is to pay my rent, mate,' he said, laughter subdued to a grin. 'It's work or the dole.' He shrugged. 'Simple as that. I don't know how you three get your money.' He looked them over, crouched among the dirty clothing and detritus flung on the floor. 'There's only a few ways I can think of. Work for your dinner, live off mummy and daddy, sign on, or steal it. Which one are you lot on?'

'We're working for the revolution,' said Tosh primly.

'Whatever we get out of the system contributes to the struggle,' said Susie.

Jack took a few steps into the room and picked up the ashtray. From it, he removed a roach which he held at arm's length like a snotty tissue.

'How does this further the revolution?'

'Get him out of here,' dismissed Anton. 'We've got work to do.'

Susie looked at Tosh. Tosh shrugged.

'Sorry,' said Susie to Jack. 'I tried.'

'You don't have to explain anything to him!' exclaimed Anton.

'What's wrong with manners!' she yelled. 'He's only trying to earn a wage.'

'Don't make excuses for blacklegs,' hissed Anton.

'He's not a blackleg,' retorted Tosh. 'Where's the strike?'

'We should support the workers...' said Susie.

'Sure!' yelled Anton. 'On the picket lines. When they're sitting-in in the factories. When they're marching on Parliament. But he's,' stabbing at Jack with his forefinger, 'servicing the toffs, the property-owning class.'

'I've also worked in schools, parks, and for the council,' said Jack, knowing too he'd also worked for some he wouldn't question too closely. 'But forget that. And I'll do you a deal.'

'Here we go,' scoffed Anton. 'More City finance.'

'Let's at least hear it,' said Susie.

'Yeh, shut up for a minute,' added Tosh.

'You poncing sellouts...' yelled Anton.

'Shut up!' his fellow anarchists shouted back. 'Shut up! Shut up for once.'

Anton threw up his hands. 'The workers divided will *always* be defeated.' He shuffled round, and turned his back on them.

'What's the deal?' said Susie.

'I fix your hot water,' said Jack, not sure whether he could or not, as he didn't know the problem, but what the hell. 'And when I've done that – you let me go round and do the estimate. And if it's accepted – you let me come and do the work.'

'We certainly need hot water,' said Susie looking at her dirty hands.

'What I'd do for a shower!' exclaimed Tosh.

Anton swivelled round. He gazed at his two mates, then at Jack, sucking his cheeks. A speck of muesli was on his lips.

'Plus two fifty,' he said.

Jack screwed up his eyes. 'What?'

The other two also turned to Anton. Susie was nodding, having caught on, Tosh was plainly puzzled.

'First fix the hot water,' explained Anton. 'It's all conditional on that. Then do the estimate but bump it up by £250 – and that goes to the cause.'

'You want me to deliberately overcharge,' said Jack, 'and give it to you?'

'You got it,' said Anton.

'That's corruption.'

'Too right. Revolutions cost,' said Anton. 'It goes in the coffers.'

'And not the ashtray?'

Susie laughed. Tosh smiled. Anton grimaced.

'£250 on top,' he said, tight-lipped. 'Or stuff it.'

'Let me have a think,' said Jack, scratching his head. They watched as he struggled. Was it corruption? No question. They'd get money for nothing. For the cause. For smokes more like. He wouldn't enquire further. But he had no other work and the mortgage was due...

'I might not get the job if I bump it up,' he said.

'You will,' said Anton.

'How do you know that?'

Anton laughed for the first time, his teeth had been smashed up somewhere.

'We won't let anyone else in,' he exclaimed.

Jack was impressed at his deviousness. He could imagine Anton as a cut-throat supermarket buyer, squeezing farmers on their milk quotas. Not a thought he shared with him. Go with the customer.

'You won't go back on this?' he said.

'You do your bit, we do ours,' said Susie.

'Vote on it,' said Jack.

'Agreed?' said Susie looking to her colleagues. The others nodded. 'Right then. I propose that if Jack fixes the hot water and adds two fifty to the estimate for the cause, then we let him get on with the job without hindrance. That's the motion. Who seconds it?'

'I second it,' said Tosh.

'We've had the discussion,' said Susie. 'So - all in favour.'

Three hands rose.

'Against.'

Jack watched in wonder as, quite mathematically, no hands rose against. It could have been a full council meeting. There were delusions here of significance. A cult, a religion.

'The proposal is passed unanimously.'

'It's a deal,' said Jack. 'I'll fix your hot water.'

Chapter 3

Jack was not the greatest plumber but he'd worked with a few and done some of the simpler jobs on his own. And he'd learnt, since he'd been a self employed builder, that an expert was someone who knew that bit more than you did. Talk as if you know, look confident and wield a big spanner.

He went into the kitchen, ignoring the dishes and pots on the units. There was no fridge or cooker, simply dirty spaces where they'd been. There was though a microwave. It reminded him of a student house he'd worked in once. The sink, like this one, full of dishes and saucepans waiting for the house fairy.

Jack turned on the cold tap. The water ran freely, splashing him as it hit the pans. He turned it off, knowing water was coming into the house. He turned on the hot tap. Nothing. Was it just this sink?

He went around the house, trying the hot water taps. In the sink of the downstairs toilet. Nothing. He went up the stairs. The hot water wasn't working in the bathroom. Susie had been following him.

'Do you know what it is?' she said.

This was the expert bit, though he'd been here before, so maybe he was one anyway. 'Water is coming into the house via the mains,' he said. 'No problem there. But the hot water isn't flowing anywhere. That's a separate system usually. The mains fills the hot water tank which will be at the top of the house. So you've either got an empty hot water tank or there's an airlock in the system which is stopping the water coming out.' He rubbed his nose, a thinking pose. 'I want to look at the hot water tank. Do you know where it is?'

'No, I don't.'

They were in the upstairs bathroom. Stains of printer's ink round the sink, dirty rags in the bath.

'There, I reckon,' said Jack looking upwards. And pointed to a square wooden panel in the ceiling. 'That'll be the loft door. And most likely where the hot water tank is.'

He'd need a ladder to get up there. And would have to go to his lock-up to get one. Should have brought one anyway, as he'd need to look at the roof. But a step ladder for now.

'You wouldn't have a ladder?' he asked, not too hopefully.

'We do,' she said eagerly. 'Or rather they do. The owner's, or whoever, in the garden shed.'

'Can you get it for me while I fetch my tools?'

'Sure.'

They went their separate ways. Jack to his van, she out the back garden. He didn't need the ladder to fix their hot water, if he was right, but would need his double extension ladder to do the estimate. He always forgot something.

Outside he breathed freely. That place was stuffy, but out here the sun was shining on anarchists, capitalists, and small builders. There was a chill in the air but it was warming with the rising sun. He left the front door open. Some fresh air wouldn't do the house any harm, though might choke the residents. Admittedly, he wasn't the tidiest of persons himself. Alison had reminded him of that too often when they were living together. And now in his own flat, he had a tendency to wait until he ran out of plates before he washed up. Though he'd sussed out the technique; don't have more crockery, pots and pans, than you need. Then the mess can't pile up too much. And besides, Mia's visits kept him tidy. Alison had threatened that Mia wasn't coming unless his place passed inspection. And that was difficult to argue with, much as he'd have liked to.

Out of the van he took his toolbox, a few plumbing bits and pieces, and a head torch for dark spaces. Across the road, out of the window of the decrepit house, an old lady had raised a curtain and was watching him. He gave her a wave and a smile. She waved back eagerly and that improved his mood. There's no need to argue with everything. Life is short enough.

Back in the bathroom, Susie was already there with the stepladder. It was old, wooden, grey, the two pieces of rope between the legs were pretty rotten. Jack put his foot on the bottom step and stomped down hard. It cracked and split in two.

'Fit for the bonfire,' said Jack. 'No wonder they left it behind.'

So tank or airlock in the pipes? He considered using a chair and trying to scramble into the loft. And break his neck. Not worth the effort. Try the airlock idea, then.

'Let's assume it isn't the tank,' he said for Susie's benefit. 'Let's shift the airlock.'

'Shall I take the ladder away?' she said.

'Yes,' he said. Then had a thought. 'Hang on a sec.' From his tool box he took out his goggles and a hammer. 'Have these.' He handed them to Susie who looked at them in puzzlement. 'Take the ladder to the patio – and smash up each step. We don't want anyone breaking their neck on it.'

'Right, Jack.'

She put on the goggles, picked up the ladder and with his help left the bathroom. He liked her. She'd called him Jack. He was already matey with one of the household. She was eager, helpful and had got him into the house in the first place. So a useful ally. Anton was the enemy. Tosh was pliable. Could go either way. He wondered which one she was sleeping with. Both? Neither? All three sleeping bags were in the room together.

Or were they too busy planning the revolution?

He checked the sink's cold tap. It was working fine, the water running fast and freely. So it must come directly off the mains. Nothing from the hot tap. Logical for an air-block. Out of the toolbox he took a length of hose, about half a metre long. He hoped it would be this easy. It was magic when it worked.

Jack connected the hose on to the cold tap nozzle and the other end on to the hot tap. Then turned on the hot tap. Of course, nothing happened. Then the cold. This was the force, and with luck it would blow out the trapped air. There was a spluttering and a gurgling. So something was happening in those far pipes.

He let it continue a while. Then turned off both taps and removed the hose. Crossing fingers, he turned on the hot water tap. After some whooshing, bits of rust spat out, then water came, full flow. He allowed it to run a while. He'd probably fixed the air blockage, but needed to check the other hot water taps in the house.

He went round the house checking all the hot water taps. Each in turn worked. He let them run a while, clearing out the pipes. The last one was in the kitchen. Outside on the patio, Susie was smashing the steps of the ladder, plainly enjoying herself in this necessary destruction. He put his head out of the kitchen door.

'You've got hot water.'

'Great!' She flew into the kitchen yelling to the house, 'We've got hot water! He's fixed it. I bags first shower.'

Two inky men came out of a side room where a machine was rhythmically whirring. Susie was already running up the stairs.

'I'll switch on the thermostat!'

Chapter 4

Jack had been round the house, checking off items that needed repairing. Mostly small stuff, loose boards here and there, a shaky banister, stuck windows, handles on doors that didn't work, a down-pipe coming off the wall, guttering that was losing contact with the roof. He needed to check the roof itself and the loft, so he'd need his ladder to finish the estimate. He decided to pop next door, see Jan and tell her what was happening. She was in touch with Terry more than he was.

Susie had taken her shower, her face bright, her hair frizzy, but was now getting dirty again as she was working with the others on the printer, a machine that had seen better days but still worked, in a very inky mode. Jack, as he wandered that room noting repairs, suspected someone was glad to get the machine off their hands.

Could he leave his tools in the squat? With all their 'Up the Workers' stance, the revolution could easily justify liberating a hammer and screwdriver or two. So he packed everything away and headed next door with his toolbox. He might as well do Jan's few jobs and earn some money today instead of this spec stuff.

He'd gone down the path on to the pavement and was turning towards Jan's, when there was a shout from the house on the other side. He turned and saw standing on the front step a middle aged Asian woman in a red salwar kameez and matching hijab.

'Mr Builder!' she called.

'Yes, madam,' he called back. 'What can I do for you?'

He headed in her direction, stopping at her gate, thinking there might be work in this, best behaviour called for.

'Amina spoke to you this morning,' she said in a slight Asian accent. Her face was rounded and she was tending towards plumpness. There were fading mendhi patterns on her hands.

'A nice young lady,' he said, though even as he said it he was unsure he should be complimenting a young Muslim woman. But the woman merely smiled, so he went on, 'She said your patio needed some work.'

'Yes,' said the woman. 'She phoned me a little while ago. And I thought I would catch you.' Adding more quietly, 'as you're working next door in that squatted house.'

Jack had come down her checkered tiled path to her front door.

'Not the easiest place to work,' he said quietly, indicating next door with a slight throw of his head.

She put a hand to her mouth and almost whispered. 'What are they like?'

Jack put down his toolbox by the bottom step. 'Difficult,' he said. 'I'm trying not to get involved. I work for the owner, but I had a lot of hassle getting in there.'

'I saw you on the front step,' said the woman. 'You were there a long time.'

'I had to persuade them that the repairs were to their advantage,' said Jack. 'I told them it was nothing to do with me who lived there.'

The woman shook her head and sucked her lips. 'We have been so worried about that house. It has been empty for so long.'

'I don't understand the property market,' said Jack. 'Houses should be lived in.'

'Quite right,' she said. 'Would you mind looking at our patio?'

'I'll do it now,' he said. 'If that's convenient.'

'I hoped you would,' she said. 'Please come this way.'

Jack came up the few steps to the front door. There were

shoes in the hallway near the door in a stepped shoe-rack. He had worked before for Muslims so knew the drill. He put down his toolbox and, without being asked, undid his shoelaces and took off his boots.

'Can I leave my toolbox here?'

'Certainly.'

He put down the box by the shoe-rack and carried his boots with him through the hallway. A smell of garlic and curry reminded him that he was hungry. It was mid morning already. He followed the woman into the kitchen at the back of the house where an elderly lady was chopping vegetables at the table.

'Hello,' he said.

She smiled and said Hello back in a strong Asian accent. The two women spoke briefly in their own language and the old lady nodded, from which he gathered that it was OK him being here. He knew in stricter Muslim houses, his being present without the man of the house would be out of the question.

She led him out the back door to the garden. Jack sat on the back step and slipped on his boots. He did them up in a loose bow as he knew that he'd be taking them off again to go back in. But this was the way and it had made sense when it had been explained to him. Walking the soil of the street all around the house was seen to be foul. It couldn't be argued otherwise, Jack knew. It was a western dirty habit.

The patio had an ornate large metal table with chairs to match. There was a wooden bench with some oriental ornamentation. Along the sides of the patio were various large pots with plants at different stages of growth. In the garden itself there were crocuses past their best and daffodils gleaming in the sunshine.

Jack walked about the patio, looking at its condition. Some of the flagstones were broken, others chipped.

'What do you think?' she said. 'My daughter is getting

married in two weeks. And a lot of the guests will be coming here.'

'Amina?' he asked.

'No, my eldest daughter, Inaya.'

Jack paced across from fence to fence, although he'd already worked out what could be done. He counted pavings and had a rough working of the width and length of the patio. He made some jottings in his notebook.

'Would you like a cup of tea?' said the woman.

He didn't really want one, as he was going to Jan's. How much tea could you take? Susie had made some at the anarchists', a sort of celebration that hot water was back. It was polite to say yes whether you wanted it or not. Expected. Somewhat cross cultural.

'Yes, please,' he said.

She went in while he sat at the table to do his calculations. How many paving stones, how much sand and cement, and the carting away of refuse, the time the job would take him.

She returned in a few minutes with a cup of tea and a piece of rich cake. He was grateful for the cake. The tea was sugared and he'd rather it wasn't, but it was tea and well meant. He complimented her on the cake. It was stuffed with dates and sultanas, a good chunky mid morning bite, filling. Jack was looking out at the garden as he ate. Its openness. The garden was long, south facing, all the better for the planets and the moon he thought, and abutted on to another long garden on the other side of the back fence. No trees but shrubs against the fences.

'Be a good place for a telescope,' he mused. 'This patio.'

'My husband has one,' she said.

'What sort?' he said, immediately interested.

She waved her hands. 'I've no idea,' she said. 'It's just a very long one.'

'A refractor,' said Jack.

'It is,' she exclaimed. 'I remember that word. Five inches... Does that sound right?' He nodded eagerly. 'Don't ask me anything else.'

'Sounds like a good one,' he said. 'I've one myself. Not as good. But I won't bore you. Back to your patio. You can either have the cheap job for £150, where I replace just the damaged paving stones. Or the expensive one, £750, where I replace the lot.'

'Which do you advise?' she said.

He shrugged. 'It's up to you. Personally, I'd go for the cheap one,' he said. 'The majority of the paving stones are fine; why dump them? The problem is the new ones will be a different colour unless I can find some second hand ones. Though, a place I was at a few months back, they painted them all different colours – and they looked amazing.'

Just then a middle aged Asian man stepped out into the garden from the kitchen door. He was short and portly, bald on top with a grey fringe round the sides, wearing a well-cut navy blue pin-striped suit.

'My husband,' said the woman.

'I hear you have a refractor,' said Jack to the man.

'Yes,' he said, at once as eager as Jack had been. 'An Altair 130. Do you know about scopes?'

'I know that's impressive,' said Jack. 'I've an 8 inch Newtonian Explore.'

'I'd be interested how they compare,' said the man thoughtfully. 'An 8 inch Newtonian with a 5 inch refractor.... That'd be an interesting competition. Saturn's out tonight. Why not come to dinner? The girls would love a telescope party.'

'Sounds marvellous,' said Jack. 'I only live up the road, across Woodgrange. But I'd have to bring my daughter. She's only 12, but knows her stuff when it comes to astronomy.'

'Bring her along by all means. We'll have a great time.

I'm keen to compare scopes. And two of them, that's almost a club. I see you've got some tea and some of my wife's cake. Heavy.' He laughed. 'It would feed an army crossing the Himalayas.'

The woman said something in their language to him. The man shrugged and said with a smile in English, 'The more the merrier.' He said to Jack, 'We've invited the famous author from number 70.' He turned to his wife and said in English, 'What's her books?'

'Mimi the Space Cat. Amina asked me to invite her which I did half an hour ago.'

'I used to read them to my daughter,' said Jack.

'Space Cat,' said the man rubbing his hands. 'Totally apt for a star party. And we'll get to know the neighbours too.' He said more quietly, 'But we won't invite the squatters... What do you make of them?'

'They're anarchists,' said Jack. 'They want a revolution. Tomorrow.'

'Such a nice house,' said the man sadly, shaking his head. 'I am sure they're ruining it.' He looked at his watch. 'But I must run off. I just popped in to get some papers.' He put his hand out. 'Aklis Choudhury.'

Jack shook his hand. 'Jack Bell. I'll bring the quote along tonight.'

'Must be off,' said Mr Choudhury as they parted. 'Good to meet you, Jack. I look forward to this evening. Let's hope the sky stays clear.' And he left them.

Jack stayed a few minutes longer to eat his cake. Then said his goodbyes and headed for Jan's.

Chapter 5

Jack fixed a new washer in the tap in Jan's bathroom. It was a simple job. He always kept a range of washers as dripping taps were common enough, easily fixed and people always grateful. It was simply a matter of turning the water off where it came into the house, then undoing the tap, removing the old washer and putting in the new. Not rocket science. And not particularly skilful, just the right tools, a little knowledge and a washer.

The other job was her back door. It was difficult to open and shut, sticking in the jamb. He could see clearly where. At the top, for a couple of feet down, it was tight. There was no help for it, he'd have to take the door off and plane it. Jack went out to his vehicle and brought in the wedges that he'd made up for himself so he could take off doors single-handed. Without the wedges under the door, all the weight on the last screw could rip the doorjamb.

The door off, he took it out on to the patio and leaned it against the wall that ran across the area, the edge to be planed upwards. The garden was as long as the Choudhurys' but had a couple of tall trees at the back. Not so good for a telescope session. Pity. Be at its worst in summer when the trees were in leaf, being south facing, a lot of time you'd lose the planets in their foliage. Frustrating. He wondered whether Jan had a gardener as it was in good trim. That looked like a vegetable patch. Not much on it, but some bushes, probably fruit, and naked bean poles.

Jack kept his planes sharp with his carborundum stone. A blunt plane tore instead of running smoothly. It was satisfying shaving off wood in curls, pure carpentry, the smell of the wood, the run of the body taking the plane along the surface. The job itself took only a few minutes. Most of the time was taken up by taking down the door, marking up, tidying the wood shavings and putting back the door. Jan told him to put the shavings in the compost bin.

He was wondering what to charge her. Here she was, making him lunch. He'd had two coffees from her. What, 30 quid for this? It was what he'd normally charge. Both jobs had only taken about forty minutes, and he was on the spot, so no travel time. But he'd done a good job. And like Bob said, don't be too cheap. Besides, house like this, no kids, she can afford it. It was probably nothing to her. He'd drop her in an invoice. More businesslike.

When he'd done it, the door back up and swinging freely, they had lunch in the kitchen. She told him she was making it for herself anyway and it was a change to have company. They had Welsh rarebit, which she decorated with sliced tomato and black olives. She brought out coleslaw and salad from the fridge.

As they ate, he told her about the anarchists.

'I was surprised you got in,' she said.

'It wasn't easy,' he said, and he gave her more details on the machinations next door once he was inside.

She was listening intently, staring at him. He wondered whether she was trying to make him uncomfortable or signalling something else, either way, he was restless as he recounted his dealings with the anarchists. She was amused by their arguments amongst themselves, and he wondered whether to tell her about the two fifty pay-off they wanted. But he decided to, as he wasn't getting it, simply the anarchists taking advantage of their position.

'Sneaky bastards,' she said.

'I don't like it,' he said.

She shrugged, pushing her hair behind her ears.

'If it stops the house falling to bits...' she said. 'I doubt Terry will notice.'

'I was thinking of telling him. When I email the estimate.' Her eyes widened. 'Why not? It makes it clear that whoever else gets the job, if they even let them in, they'll have to pay the fee too.'

'Terry might not believe you,' she said. 'She might think you are just bumping up the estimate. Builders being builders.' She smiled teasingly.

'It's a pain,' he said blowing out his cheeks. 'I either play straight and explain what the anarchists have demanded. Or I bury their rake off. But to do that I have to bump my prices up to cover it. Or invent work.'

He took a bite of the cheesy toast. Some fancy cheese that she'd lightly peppered. Very nice. And salad too, giving his system a spring clean.

'I'll think about it,' he said. 'I've still got to get my ladders and look at the roof and loft before I can finish the estimate.'

'How much do I owe you?' she said.

'Thirty quid,' he said quickly. Then added, 'Cash. Or £37 on invoice.'

'I'll give you cash. Simpler.'

It was a minor tax fiddle. Easy for small jobs. Cash and no VAT paid. He couldn't do it all the time or the tax people got suspicious. But these little jobs... Though interestingly, he'd given her the choice – and it was she who was fiddling the tax really. He didn't get the money, just collected it for the government and passed it on. Really he shouldn't do it. And in her case, why? If the well-off didn't pay tax then the poor paid more. It was habit. Trying to keep his prices down.

'I hear you've been invited to the Choudhurys',' he said to get off the subject.

She sighed. 'I don't know why I said yes to that. Could be a chore. I'm useless with neighbours. Though they can be useful for taking in parcels. Might be a very boring evening. All manners and smiles.'

'I'm going too.'

'How come?'

'I was called over to look at their patio. Needs some work; they've a wedding coming up. And I met Mr Choudhury, and we talked telescopes. He's got one, I've got one. Refractor versus reflector. Man talk.'

'I've got a telescope,' she said.

He was taken aback. Though why he should be when his own daughter was keen on astronomy... Habit.

'I'm a member of Loughton Astronomical Society,' she said. 'I thought Space Cat and all that, I'd better learn some astronomy. It means I don't get things totally wrong.'

'What have you got?'

'A Celestron 150 Massutov Cassegrain. What's yours?'

'Eight inch Newtonian Explore.'

'Interesting. Want to see mine?'

They'd more or less finished lunch and left the remnants on the table. He followed her up the stairs where there were illustrations of Space Cat on the wall along with a couple of posters with the featured cat astronaut and pals, strange planets and goofy aliens. The landing had a soft-piled, cream carpet. Great for walking around barefoot.

She took him into the bedroom. There was the telescope, and there was the bed.

The telescope was quickly forgotten.

Chapter 6

Anton had gone out. One of his mysterious visits. Tosh and Susie had a shower together. And then made love in the upstairs room on the thick-piled rug. Usually they did it in the evenings, when Anton was writing. He always wrote for a couple of hours each day but wouldn't let either of them look at it, or even talk about it. They guessed it was some theoretical tome.

Afterwards, they were peckish but there wasn't much in the kitchen. Some stale bread, a small piece of cheese, one egg, barely enough milk for two cups of tea.

'We should get some money off the builder,' said Tosh as he nibbled the bread with his tea.

'He has to put the estimate in first,' she said, 'before he gets any cash. How much have we got?'

They emptied their pockets and the change jar and counted up.

'Two pounds 73,' he said. 'Not even enough for a pizza.'

'You could ask your parents for a couple of thou,' she said.

'I wouldn't get it,' he said, 'not after last time.' He laughed at the memory. 'Not unless I signed up for the Tory party and got a job in a City bank.'

'Well, at least you're clean. That would please your mum,' she said. 'I hardly remember you so clean. But your clothes are somewhat smelly and your teeth are yellow.'

'We need toothpaste,' he said, rubbing his teeth with a finger. 'Yours are yellow too.'

'What can we get for two 73?' she said.

'Bread...'

'I'm sick of bread.'

'And peanut butter.'

'Oh, that's a good idea. Why don't you go out and get it and I'll wash up.'

'Anton will have a go at you,' he said. 'Traditional bourgeois roles.'

'You wash up then.'

'He'd say washing up is bourgeois whoever does it.'

She laughed, her bush of hair shaking over her forehead, then tapped him on the shoulder. 'Shall we see what he's been writing?'

'An update of *Das Kapital* I bet,' he said. 'You look, I'm too hungry. I'm going out shopping.'

He gathered up the coins and pocketed them, gave Susie a peck on the cheek which he could do as Anton wasn't present – and headed out.

She thought, what shall I do – wash up or look at Anton's opus? Wash up first or she wouldn't do it. That was the way of it. So easy to postpone.

The sink was full. One reason why no one washed up; there was no room in the sink. She took everything out and put it on one side. Then half filled the sink with warm water. Lovely warm water. There wasn't any washing up liquid or a sponge, so she used soap and her fingers, leaving the tap running slowly to rinse off the items once clean.

She quite liked washing up although she knew as a woman it was demeaning, but it was warm, automatic and, whatever Anton said, useful. And she could think. She thought of contacting her parents. But the chore of a phone call. The inquisition she'd get. At what point in her life would they stop treating her like a child? It was her life, let her make her own mistakes.

Her parents had never challenged anything. They'd slipped into gentle capitalism as if that was all there ever could be. Like programmed robots. After she'd dropped out of university, she found she couldn't talk to them any more.

Why had she chosen English literature anyway? Just to please her mother. Stuffy, middle class authors writing about the stuffy middle class for stuffy middle class readers. It was suffocating. Burn Jane Austen and her marriage plans for little women, her gossip and dances, and the invisible servants traipsing in and out with tea trays. And all the time a war with Napoleon going on but you would never know it with all the trips to Bath and the assessing of incomes and the nuances of class, class, class.

The washing up was done, dripping on the draining board. No need to wipe it. She quite regretted having finished it all. The process had given her thoughts of Jane Austen and home, a vision of her parents in their armchairs watching *Pride and Prejudice*. Maybe she should write them a letter, but then she'd need a stamp. Not an email as that would start a correspondence. She simply wanted to say, I am all right, don't worry. And ask if they were all right too. For she did care, even if five minutes of their company brought her out in boils.

She went into the big room. That was what they called it. There was no furniture in it, so you could hardly call it a sitting room. They had a print room. The kitchen of course. And the soft piled carpet room upstairs which was hardly a bedroom as they never slept in it. It was the shagging room. That made her laugh. A room in the house with that sole purpose. Like the billiard room or the smoking room. Functional.

This room could do with a tidy up. A window open would not come amiss, but they felt they needed to keep out the street and its stink of bourgeois ownership spreading on the breeze like flu germs. She crouched on Anton's sleeping bag. It smelt of sweat, zoo-ey, straw odours. Hers probably wasn't much better; you got used to your own smells. Class really was about dirt. They'd discussed that for hours one night. The further away from the dirt you are, the higher up the pecking order. At the top, flunkies washed your sheets, picked up your underwear, scrubbed and vacuumed, cleaned and cleaned, so the toffs could sparkle as they stepped out of their chauffeur driven cars. Not knowing one end of a broom from the other. Which reminded her, they needed one. What an argument that would be, diverting funds from the cause. Or maybe she'd just steal a few quid from the box and buy one. Anton would never notice.

The stack of papers was a little way down the sleeping bag, several inches thick, bound in an elastic band. She looked at the top page, handwritten to perhaps three quarters down in Anton's almost indecipherable scrawl. She tried reading it. Was the handwriting more impenetrable than the prose? She supposed this was part of a long argument and she was coming in somewhere near the end, or the middle, depending how long he cared to go on for.

She put it back in his sleeping bag. Anton could keep his secrets. She hadn't even taken the elastic band off. Of course, it might be better when printed up in a book. Spaced, a decent font, paragraphs even, with headings and footnotes. Or it might be just as dull. She wouldn't say anything to Anton. It kept him quiet, gave her and Tosh some uninterrupted time. And maybe it was brilliant and she was just too stupid to understand its dialectic. Though she suspected it was babble, endless babble, packed out with stock phrases. She'd picked out 'proletariat' three times, and 'means of production' a couple of times. Perhaps a computer could write it, given the expressions and let run. But then she and Tosh wouldn't get time off.

Something was under her buttocks. Something hard, in the sleeping bag, right down the end. She hesitated going down there. Too Anton, sweaty, all the fluid, gassy expulsions of his body. They needed a washing machine, no matter what Anton thought about dirt and class. Why shouldn't the working class be as clean as aristocrats? She unpeeled the sleeping bag gingerly, holding her breath as she went further in, down into the lower depths. And, when the sleeping bag was all but turned inside out, she found a gun.

It was weighty and real. Not that she knew much about guns. This though was metal, no plastic child's toy. She had no idea whether it was loaded. In films she'd seen them pack something into the handle which presumably was full of bullets. And wasn't there a safety catch to stop you accidentally shooting your foot off?

Anton was up to something. That was plain enough. You didn't have a gun to shoot mice. A cat would be better. She'd like a cat. No doubt Anton would shoot it for some twisted reason. There had to be ammunition somewhere. Though maybe there was enough already in it.

What a thing to find. A killing machine. It had no other purpose. A knife, you could at least slice carrots with. A handgun was for shooting people.

They were illegal. Very illegal. For good reason. They were for knocking people off. Sometimes for scaring them as they thought you might be crazy enough to kill them. There had to be some ammunition somewhere. Anton wouldn't just have a gun by itself. He'd want to make a big bang. Make capitalists jump before he shot them.

She found several boxes at the bottom of his rucksack, and was looking at them when Tosh returned.

Chapter 7

'Stop grinning,' said Jan.

She was dressed, hair tied back in a pony tail, he was lying naked on the wide bed, flat out staring at the ornate ceiling rose round the lamp, or at least in that direction. He sat up lazily, the smile plastered on his face.

'Was that a surprise?' she said, already at the door.

'I only came up to see your telescope,' he said.

'It's over there.' She pointed to the corner, at the bulky instrument on a stand. 'Forget it for now. I want you to see my sketches. I'll be in my workroom.'

And she left him.

Jack swung his legs on to the floor; he could so easily have a nap. But things to do. He looked around the room, having not seen much of it earlier. Classy. Soft carpet and Mediterranean blue, thick curtains, almost to the floor. He could just make out his head in the large, oblong mirror on the wall over the mantelpiece, beyond the foot of the bed. Beside it, an abstract painting, about a metre square, wild splashes of primary colours. Did people really buy that stuff, or was it hers, or a mate's? Maybe she was hiding it away up here.

Though it could be she liked it. He stared at the painting, hoping its secret would leap out at him. Streaks of blue, yellow and red on white. A kid could have done it in primary school. Some of Mia's early daubs weren't so different. Perhaps he should get them framed. He'd always suspected modern art was a con. Enough people shout in praise, and then the suckers buy. It's in the collectors' interest to say that a photo of Marilyn Monroe, with a splash of yellow, is genius, worth millions. Or maybe it just was, and he was an ignorant builder.

And there was the telescope, one of those 6 inch reflectors, something or other Cassegrain. A sturdy stand and a go-to handset. If he started looking at it, then he'd never get away. He glanced at his watch. Oh dear, that was a stretched lunch hour. Telescopes this evening. Get something done this afternoon. At least he'd done Jan's job, and he must finish the estimate for the Asian family at 72. Get it out and away, and hopefully accepted so he could get some money in on account and begin working.

Move, move, you randy ape!

A few minutes later he joined Jan in her workroom downstairs. She had sketches on the floor; he noted she used it like a huge drawing table, spreading stuff around so she could see them all. But these weren't the Space Cat pictures that he'd seen earlier but an assortment of cartoon builders, funny tools, ladders, a van, scaffolding with crazy builders clambering up.

She said, 'I want to move on from Space Cat. I've one more to do. I'll do it somehow or other and that's that. Fifteen years of the cat in space, I've had enough of it. It's money for jam, my agent says. But I don't need jam. I need something to get me up in the morning.' She circled round the drawings on the floor. 'It was you in your overalls turning up this morning. Me, saying I'd do your website as I'd been such a cow. I started roughing pictures for it. Then before I knew it, I had this idea for a series. Three builders. Sparks, Chippie and Brickie. That one's Sparks.' She indicated a sketch of a monkey in overalls, a pencil behind its ear, taking a length of wire from a roll with pliers in the other hand. 'That's Brickie.' Brickie was a huge gorilla, standing by a cement mixer, a brick in one hand, a trowel in the other, beside a wall he was building. 'And that's Chippie.' Chippie was human in overalls, and had suggestions of Jack. He was planing the edge of a door.

'I'll sue,' he said.

'I'll dedicate the first book to *Jack of All Trades*.'

'Will that do me any good?'

'Afraid not. Kids don't employ builders. Though...' she flicked her finger as an idea came, 'I could put the cartoon figures on your van.'

'Lord God save me,' he exclaimed. 'I'd get the meat and two veg taken out of me from here to forever. Leave my van alone.'

'OK.' She seemed a little saddened at the rejection.

'Why...' he began looking at her various sketches, 'a monkey and a gorilla, when you've got the whole animal kingdom?'

'You need hands!' she sang, waving her fingers like Al Jolson. 'To build with, to hold things. You might have noticed,' she added.

'Your Space Cat didn't.'

'No cats allowed,' she said firmly.

'How about a beaver for a carpenter?'

'There's a thought.' She picked up one of the Jack likenesses, somewhat exaggerated in the size of ears and nose. 'A beaver? Maybe. But I do feel some affection for this one.'

'You'll get over it.'

'Likely I will. Anyway, I shall play around with sketches for the next couple of days. Try some more animals. How about some seagull roofers? A girl would be a good idea... Get away from the male stereotype. This needs some thinking out. Coffee?'

'I must pick my ladders up and finish the estimate next door.'

'One thing before you go. I'd like to be your mate.'

'What?'

'Isn't that the expression? Bricklayer's mate and all that. For the job next door, say just the mornings. To give me ideas.'

It came to him what she meant. Not a friend or lover. A workmate.

'I can't pay you,' he said.

'I'll be an unpaid intern. A gofer. An apprentice. It's experience, Jack. Look, I need ideas. Next door is perfect for me, and you'll be doing a variety of jobs. I'll be bubbling with inspiration.'

'The anarchists won't like it.'

'Suppose I simply turn up on day one?'

'We could try it. But there'll be no work if I don't get the estimate in,' he said sharply.

'Off you go.' She dismissed him with a flip of the hand. 'See you this evening.'

Chapter 8

'What's this?' said Susie.

She and Tosh were in the big room when Anton returned. She had the gun in her lap.

'A gun?' said Anton with mock surprise.

Susie rolled her eyes.

'We know what it is,' said Tosh. 'What's it for?'

'Shooting fascists,' said Anton with a wide grin.

'Any particular ones?' asked Susie. She pointed the gun at him, both arms outstretched as she'd seen in the movies, one eye closed. 'Is it loaded?'

'Luckily for me, no.'

'What's it for?' said Tosh.

'For a job.'

He was the only one of them that hadn't showered when the hot water came on, as if the ink on his hands, the streak on his face were badges of honour. Evidence of real work. Sweat and grime. His jeans were lived in, another skin, with their sheen of grease.

'Are you going to tell us, or do we have to guess?' said Susie. The gun was still pointed at Anton, following him as he moved about the room. She wouldn't pull the trigger, just in case he was wrong.

'Prince William,' said Anton, turning to face them. 'Prominent member of the royal parasites. We're going to kidnap him.'

'Prince William?' exclaimed Tosh. 'Honest?'

'Honest,' said Anton. 'Second in line to the throne. Who could be better?'

'He's popular,' said Susie, contemplating the very idea.

'A leech,' said Anton, 'with a pretty wife, exemplifying

the lumpen proletariat's worship of the powerful and good looking.'

'He has security with him all the time,' said Tosh.

'So he has,' exclaimed Anton. 'I'd quite forgotten that. But ah yes, one of them is ours.'

'Nice one,' said Susie. 'Makes a change from the cops infiltrating us.'

'Our guy could just shoot him,' said Tosh.

'And get shot himself?' Anton shook his head vigorously. 'This is not a suicide mission, Tosh. We leave that to the Islamists who go to heaven when they're blown to bits. With seventy virgins and fountains of sherbet. Sadly, we get zilch. So the aim is Heaven on Earth.'

'By kidnapping William,' said Susie, 'and the workers will then rise... Hallelujah!'

'We're not idiots, Susie,' said Anton, giving her his cracked toothed smile. 'But with videos of the prince telling the truth about his parasitical family and the capitalist system in general...'

'It will gather wall to wall media,' said Tosh enthused.

'Exactly,' said Anton. 'Next week, he's giving a speech at the Grosvenor Hotel to business leaders and Tory crawlers. I'll be there. With that gun. And with a few others. But in the meantime...' He stared out the back window, at roofs beyond the garden, at budding trees, at the sky, at Heaven on Earth.

Susie was irritated. Anton always did this. Knowledge was power. It shouldn't be like this, one person dishing it out like soup to the homeless.

Anton turned back to his waiting audience. 'To make the operation work, cash is needed for various accoutrements. A chauffeur driven limousine, reservations and meals at the hotel, posh suits and shoes. You are more familiar with that sort of thing, Tosh, I'm sure. So, I volunteered us lot to get the cash needed.'

'How?' said Tosh.

'We're doing a bank job. Wednesday.'

Chapter 9

Jack was at the top of his double extension ladder checking the front roof. Four rungs extended over the guttering which gave him plenty of handhold as he looked over the roof. He always used a stand-off on his ladders when doing roof work. Or rather, he always did these days. Once, only once, he'd let his ladder lean against the roof guttering, and it came away with a judder while he was at the top. Luckily, he had a mate on the ground as the ladder slipped, so fortunately he was able to hold on to the roof, while his mate pushed the ladder back up. And he was able to get down, very shaken, but without injury.

The metal stand-off clipped over a rung and pressed against the brickwork a couple of feet below the guttering. He made sure it was firm before climbing. There was a sandbag at the foot so the ladder wouldn't slip. Check and check again. You're on your own up there.

There were leaves in the gutter from the autumn. He could remove them now, but he hadn't got the job yet. And Terry wasn't getting any work done for nothing. And there should be a wire cage where the gutter met the down pipe to stop leaves blocking it. A few tiles on the roof had shifted and would need to be put back in place. There were damp patches on ceilings, the loose tiles the likely sources. Or the lead flashing that was coming away at the edges. He should check the chimney pots, but that would have to wait until he'd got his roof ladder. Always something forgotten. Sex in the afternoon, rushing about. But why not put it on the estimate: *check and make good pots*. Stick in some figure to cover it.

He climbed down.

Jack took his ladder through the house and set it up from the patio to check the back roof. Susie and Tosh came out, curious. He noted how much cleaner they were. Though not Anton who was quite pungent but obviously didn't give a damn.

They'd got used to Jack coming and going the morning and afternoon. And he'd won Susie and Tosh's confidence when he'd fixed the hot water, though Anton still looked at him in distrust. He wondered really what they had to hide, what on earth was so important in this Forest Gate house. Earlier, he'd looked at one of the leaflets they'd been printing. It was to support a strike in Hackney. He couldn't argue with the gist of it, though the language was wild, as if it was a major step to world revolution, instead of just helping some guys who were badly treated.

Tosh had seen him reading it.

'Fancy coming?' he said.

'Working,' said Jack.

Tosh accepted that. He was perhaps the least hardline of the group.

Jack said, 'You're not from round here.'

Tosh laughed. 'Everyone spots that. I wonder how.'

'It's that la-di-da accent. You could be reading the news on the Beeb.'

'This accent cost my folks twenty thou a year – and I wish to hell I could get rid of it,' said Tosh with a shrug. 'Blame Winchester and 18 months at Jesus, Cambridge, studying medieval history.'

Jack chuckled. 'Not a lot of help to the workers.'

'You could say that,' said Tosh, 'but serfdom and the Peasants' Revolt confirms you get nothing without a fight.'

'They met at Mile End,' said Jack. 'I remember that from school. We went there and saw some mural to commemorate the 600th anniversary of the Peasants' Revolt. And then they went on to Smithfields where Wat Tyler was killed.'

'I'm impressed,' said Tosh. 'The King, Richard II, met them there, made all sorts of promises. So the peasants went peacefully back to their villages. And the lords welshed on the lot, hanging and slaughtering...'

'What should the peasants have done?'

Tosh grinned. 'Kidnapped Richard for a start.'

Jack put his ladder up from the patio and climbed. Much the same as the front, some shifted tiles, a few broken. Though there was a skylight. That was puzzling as it must be from the loft and that was virtually inaccessible. It might make more sense when he got in the loft.

Having looked at front and back roofs, Jack took down his double extension ladder, and went up to the bathroom with his stepladder to check the loft. There were two filthy towels on the floor. Did no one pick anything up round here? He threw them in the bath to get them out of the way of his ladder.

The ladder set up, Jack climbed as high as he needed to push up the square panel in the ceiling. It was somewhat stiff and needed a good heave. He shifted the board to one side. Jack wore a head torch, which at first he thought he wouldn't need as he spotted a light switch, but it didn't work. Either the bulb had gone or there was a problem with the electrics. He scrambled into the loft, torch full on. The area was large, covering all the rooms and hallway on the top floor. There were floorboards over the area, which was good, as walking on rafters could be hazardous. And there was the skylight he'd seen from outside. It brought some light in which died to almost complete blackness by the eaves.

He walked around the space, head torch on, able to stand upright under the ridge of the roof, but having to bend down to a crawl at the edge. There was evidence of damp here and there, which he'd suspected from ceiling stains in the top rooms. An empty house can deteriorate pretty quickly once water begins to get in. Some squatters he'd known were house-proud and wouldn't allow this. The current occupants seemed to delight in the house rotting over them. He could see the logic if property was theft.

He wondered why the loft had floorboards and a light. It hardly made sense with such poor access. Unless it was a half project, someone had the idea to make the loft a useable space, a room perhaps, then changed their mind because of the expense, or moved out.

But anyway, he was done here. He needed to get home and make his notes into an estimate for Terry. And hope he'd find it acceptable.

Chapter 10

When Jack got home, Mia was there. She was sitting on the sofa watching TV, her school bag dumped on the floor, her coat and navy blue jumper on top of it.

'How was school?'

'Awful.' Her face was grumpy and heavy, her body slumped. 'Why can't Mum stay in one place?'

'I thought you didn't like Brighton.'

The show on TV was cartoons for kids half Mia's age. It was flashy and blary. Creatures jumping all over the place screaming. He went to sit next to her on the sofa.

'I didn't at first,' she said. 'I didn't know anyone. Then it began to get better. Mum must have noticed. So we moved.'

'To get a better job.'

'The school's crap.'

A frog on TV was braining a crocodile with a huge log. Red stars were flying out of its head.

'What's crap about it?'

'Why a girls' school in the first place? How old fashioned can you get? There's only five white girls in our class.'

'Why's that bad?'

'Everyone is so cliquey. The Asian girls stick together, talking about weddings and family get togethers. And the black girls, it's all clubs and rap music. And the white kids are stupid.'

'What's your teacher like?'

'She hates me.'

It was hard to deal with this tale of woe. The friends she'd started to make in Brighton she'd lost. And had none here. If only Alison would stay put. It couldn't be good for a kid, being carted here and there. But what could he do? It was done, and Alison hadn't consulted him. She'd got a job as head teacher in a London school. Promotion. Hopefully she'd stick around a while, but her movements were outside his control.

The crocodile had swallowed the frog. No, it hadn't. The frog was being shot out in a sneeze like a cannon ball... Yellow stars this time.

'Do you fancy a telescope party?' he said.

'Where?'

He noticed at once she was alerted. A little eagerness he should be able to fan. He turned off the TV. She glowered.

'I was watching.'

'Crap cartoons,' he said.

'That's what going to a crap school does to you. You regress.'

'Do you want to know about the telescope party?'

She considered it. He knew that she did, but didn't want to appear enthusiastic.

'Where, with who and what instruments?' she said.

'An Asian family across Woodgrange. The father's got a six inch refractor, there's mine, and the woman a few doors away has a 6 inch, Massu... Massu – what's the word...?'

'Massutov Cassegrain,' said Mia. 'Celestron, is it?'

'Yes, with goto gizmos.'

'Where's your astronomy mag? Let's see what's about. What time is moonrise?' She got up, her energy lifted, and went to the window. 'It's quite clear out... Three scopes. I've not seen through a six inch refractor.'

'We're to be there seven thirty,' he said. 'Dinner with them first. I bet the mother's a great cook. They always put on a spread when they've got guests.'

Mia had been looking through the pile of magazines in the corner.

'Where's the latest *Sky at Night*?'

'Probably in my bedroom.' She was about to go and get

it. 'Leave it there for now. You have to get your homework done. Right away.'

'Bollocks.'

'Don't talk like that.' He stared at her, aghast.

'Why not? The girls at school do.'

'I bet they don't.'

'You just want to hear them.'

'But not from you. Get your homework done. We'll be back late. Much later than your mother likes. So get down to work. I've got an estimate to send out before I leave. And I need a shower...'

'So do I.'

'Homework first.'

There was a hint of rebellion which gave a glimmer of years to come, but instead she tipped the contents of her bag on to the carpet and searched through her workbooks. Then took a couple to the table with her bag of pens. Jack took the far end of the table with his laptop and the notebook containing today's scribblings.

After half an hour he made them some toast and marmalade.

PART TWO: STARGAZING

Chapter 11

They were a little late. Jack had been at pains to get the email estimate off before leaving. And then had to shower, while Mia was searching for the iron as she didn't want to go in her school uniform. Not that she had a lot of choice, most of her clothes being at her mother's. That didn't stop her dithering. The dinner said to her a dress, the telescope session said casual and warm. Jack knew better than to make suggestions, other than to say it might be cold in the garden. She put the dress on, took it off and finally settled on a sweatshirt, thick jumper, jeans and her Doc Martens.

'You'll have to take your boots off when we go in,' said Jack.

'I've been to Asian houses before, you know.'

He didn't know. Her and Alison's Brighton life were largely unknown to him, except when it came to Alison's turbulent love life. On that subject, Mia was forthcoming, giving him very subjective details, one part truth to three parts moan, impossible to sort which from which.

At the house door, Jack was loaded up with the telescope in his arms like a fractious infant. A hefty job, a stubby cylinder on a tripod. He was excited, almost childishly so. His own telescope was pretty good and he was eager to compare it with the others. And simply, he enjoyed talking astronomy, hopefully with a good night of stargazing. Mia was nervous, new people, all grown ups; he hoped she'd be able to cope.

Amina opened the door.

'So good of you to come,' she said with her brightest smile. 'My father loves talking astronomy. And the Space Cat lady up the road is coming too.'

'She's bringing her telescope.'

'No!' she clapped her hands. 'We'll be the astronomy centre of the East End. What am I doing keeping you at the door? Come in, come in.'

She ushered them in. There were a couple of low stools at the door, on which they sat to remove their boots.

'And this is my daughter, Mia.'

'Pleased to meet you, Mia.' Amina held out her hand and they shook.

'Pleased to meet you,' said Mia shyly.

Amina was wearing a bright red and yellow sari with a blue hijab, plainly enjoying being a hostess.

'I am so looking forward to meeting the Space Cat author,' Amina bubbled.

'Have you read them all?' said Mia.

'Yes, I have. I read all that were out when I was a kid. And now I read the others in school... All the children want her to come in.'

Amina led them through. The house was light and warm, thickly carpeted, the furniture heavy in dark wood, plus sofas and armchairs with lots of cushions with tassels. Jack left the telescope in the conservatory at the back of the house, where there was already Mr Choudhury's refractor among the low palms and ferns. He gazed at that one wistfully, knowing it couldn't have cost less than a couple of thousand. The crystal clear optics would certainly outperform his at less than a third of the price. It was a silly disappointment, he knew. Mr Choudhury could afford a better scope, but it wasn't as if he'd made it himself. It was on the market. Anyone with the money could buy it.

Jan's scope wasn't there, so he assumed she hadn't arrived yet. There was a ring on the bell. And then she was here. There was a flurry of people and introductions. Inaya, very like her sister, Mrs Choudhury, Mr Choudhury who was smiling and bouncing about like Scrooge at his resurrection. And Mr Choudhury's mother, who evidently spoke little English and said 'Please to meet you' to everyone.

'All these amazing telescopes! Capital. Capital,' exclaimed Mr Choudhury, clapping his hands just like his daughter. 'We shall have such a wonderful time. It's a good time to eat. By the time we've finished it will be fully dark and we can be out in the garden for the real event of the evening.'

He led them into the dining room.

Jan was wearing black, loose trousers and a frilly green blouse, high at the neck to suit the occasion. She had a silver comb in her hair which draped her cheeks, and wore a Wedgwood brooch of white raised figures on a blue background - a centaur picking fruit from a tree, presumably for the watching nymph. The women of the family were in bright, colourful saris and hijabs. Mr Choudhury had a dark brown, well-made suit over a white shirt. He took off his jacket as soon as he sat down at the table and put it on the back of his chair. Jack felt somewhat underdressed as he presumed the family had dressed up for the occasion, and he could see Mia looking panicky.

There were glasses by the placings for fruit juice. Jack was glad that here at least there would be no drinks palaver. He'd have no worries that someone would fill his glass automatically with wine, as if that was the default.

The food came quickly, brought in by the daughters and mother, steaming in large bowls and placed upon trivets. A mutton curry, dhal, a selection of vegetables, rice, naan bread, another meat dish that Jack couldn't catch the name of but was told it wasn't too hot. He tried some and had to douse it with yoghurt and rice.

'You haven't lived long at number 70, Jan?' asked Mr Choudhury.

'About five months,' she said. 'It was my grandmother's house; she had two houses, my sister got the one in Hornchurch and I got this.'

'So are your parents both dead?' said Inaya.

'They died about ten years ago, in that dreadful South East Asian tsunami. They were travelling round the world. Dad had only been retired for a year. They stopped off in Sumatra.' She stopped for an instant and added, 'And that was that.'

'How dreadful,' said Amina. 'It must have been a terrible time for you.'

'It was. I was living out in Essex, near Maldon, married at the time. Don't ask me about that over dinner, I might start swearing. But when I inherited the house last summer, I thought it'd be nice to come into London, be more in the swim of things, but I do miss the Blackwater. All the birds in the reeds and mud banks. But I've let my house now, so I'll be here a while.'

'Are you doing another Space Cat?' said Mia timidly.

'Have you read them?' she asked.

'Well,' said Mia. 'I've read about seven. Then I got too old.' She backtracked as if she'd said something wrong. 'But I really liked them.'

'Me too,' said Amina. 'I was reading *In the Space Café* to the children today. And they wanted to know why Click the computer is always so miserable.'

Jan smiled at the question. Jack wondered whether this was tiresome for her, though she didn't seem displeased. She wore light, subtle make-up, her hair really displayed her face. He could hardly stop looking at her.

'Click, being a computer, can't go on adventures,' explained Jan. 'She's part of the spaceship really, so she's always left behind when the others go off and explore strange planets. I think of her like a Jewish mother. You probably know the one...' She stopped for a second as if she regretted saying it, but it was too late now, she'd begun. 'How many Jewish mothers does it take to change a light bulb?'

Jack could see Mia knew this joke, but had the sense to keep it to herself.

'Tell us,' said Amina.

'None.' And added with maybe a Jewish mother accent, "Oh, don't mind me, I'll sit in the dark."

The table laughed. Mr Choudhury especially chortled and his wife gave him a look.

'Universal, universal,' he declared. 'All mothers, once their children have grown up.'

'I'd put a light bulb in, myself,' said Mrs Choudhury primly.

'Good for you,' said Jan.

'I thought,' said Mia, 'that Click was like Eeyore.'

'Oh,' said Jan, putting down her knife and fork. 'How very astute of you. I'd never thought of that. Miserable old Eeyore in Winnie the Pooh. I wonder if subconsciously I was thinking of him.'

Jack noted that Mia was pleased to be praised. Jan was good at this. Lots of practice no doubt.

'Where do you get your ideas from?' said Inaya.

Jan had told Jack at lunchtime that everywhere she went that question always came up. Never missed. In schools, festivals, someone in the audience always delivered.

'Well,' she said, 'plainly I nick them. Sometimes I know I'm doing it and sometimes it has to be pointed out to me.'

'I hear you're getting married,' said Jack to Inaya. As soon as he'd said it, he wondered whether he should have taken the focus off Jan. Did she mind or was it a release? After all, she had said she was growing tired of the Space Cat.

'In two weeks,' said Inaya beaming. 'We're having a marquee in the back garden. With a covered walkway into the house, so even if it's raining, it won't matter. Though I do hope it's not cold.'

'We're moving some of the furniture upstairs,' said Mr

Choudhury, 'to give more room.' He leaned forward, 'At one point, I was thinking of moving some of it next door, contacting the landlord, paying something, but then the squatters moved in. Tell me, Jack. You're working there. What are they like?'

'They're anarchists,' he said.

'And what sort of vegetable is that when it's in season?' snorted Mr Choudhury. 'There are those that talk and talk and can't decide anything because they refuse to have any leaders. And there are those that throw bombs. Which ones have we got?'

'The harmless sort. I think. Messy. When they leave, the house will need a good clean up. But they do argue a lot.'

'About which fork to use for the revolution?' chortled Mr Choudhury.

'They haven't got many forks. Though they were washed up today. Both of them.'

'They are very dirty,' said Mrs Choudhury screwing up her face.

'I fixed their hot water,' said Jack. 'So two of them are cleaner. One refuses to go near water.'

'They have a machine I hear sometimes through my bedroom wall, even late at night,' said Inaya. 'What is it?'

'It's a printing press.'

'Manifestos for the workers to read on the barricades,' laughed Mr Choudhury. 'Oh, what games they play! You wonder how they came to leave the real world.'

'What is the real world?' said Jack.

'Business, family, children, work.' He threw his hands in the air. 'Making your way. Becoming something. It's always nobodies who want to make a revolution, overthrow the government and create complete chaos.'

'Anarchy,' said Mrs Choudhury.

'Precisely, precisely.'

Jack might have had a few things to say about inherited

wealth and lack of equality but suspected this might cause an argument. After all, he was a guest.

'The rich are too rich,' said Amina adamantly. 'All these Russian oligarchs and Arabian sheiks buying up London... while in this very borough families are living in squalor, sleeping four to a room.'

'Meet my daughter the socialist,' said Mr Choudhury, pointing her out mock-proudly.

'I see it in school,' she went on, ignoring his jibe. 'The children who come in without breakfast, and have seconds and thirds at lunchtime because there may not be anything when they get home.'

'Because their parents are on drugs and drinking,' said Mrs Choudhury.

Jack could see the mother was angry, though he was unsure whether at the drug takers or her daughter for bringing it up at dinner where there were guests.

'Enough of politics,' said Mr Choudhury, obviously peeved. 'Forest Gate attracts riff raff.'

'Is your wife working, Jack?' said Mrs Choudhury.

'I'm divorced,' he said. 'My ex-wife is the head teacher of a primary school in Hackney.'

'Which one?' said Amina.

Jack looked to his daughter as he didn't know.

'Clapton Primary,' said Mia. 'We've just moved up from Brighton. My mum's looking at a house tonight. In Sebert Road.'

'It's where my school is,' said Amina.

Conversation continued on schools, changes in the area, and was moved quickly on when there was any danger of contention. Just as well there was no drink, thought Jack, or someone might have brought up religion and terrorism, and blamed their hosts for savagery in the Middle East.

He left them to it when they got on to house prices and tried mentally to turn off, but couldn't stop it filtering in.

Jan had two houses, he knew, one out in Essex and then she'd been given another one. They seemed to be congratulating themselves on sitting pretty.

'Silly money,' said Mr Choudhury. 'A million and a half this house is worth. So they say. What have I done for it? Up it goes, a hundred thousand or more a year. More than I can earn. Who pays?'

Jack bit his tongue, though he suspected the anarchists might have made an interesting reply.

'The poor,' said Amina. 'Those at the bottom. Isn't that the way it works? You have to have scarcity to push up the value.'

Jack was impressed. Amina was a definite lefty.

'Do you blame us for living in this house, Amina?' said her father.

'Of course not,' she said, 'but that hundred thousand a year increase in value doesn't simply rain down from the sky. It comes out of the pockets of the poor.'

'So what should we do, Amina the economist?' said her father.

She pursed her lips at the jibe and for a second hesitated before saying, 'Pay more tax.'

Mr Choudhury laughed. 'The classic socialist answer to everything.'

'So more scroungers can live off benefits,' said her mother.

Jack dared not say a word but took more curry and dhal, a bit of naan.

'Did you see that programme?' said Jan. 'With that awful family. All those people who don't want to work. Their kids all developing the something for nothing culture. They get up at noon, order pizzas and watch TV all afternoon.'

'And that family with sixteen children!' exclaimed Inaya. 'The amount they were getting! And the wife smoking, the father gambling and drinking...'

'It isn't typical,' said Jack unable to stop himself. 'They pick the most extreme cases, in order to get everyone yelling. When I was unemployed, I wasn't scrounging. I simply couldn't get any work. And I certainly couldn't afford any take-away pizzas. I bet the TV company gave them the money for it.'

'I wouldn't scrounge,' said Inaya adamantly. 'I'd stack shelves in Tesco's if I had to.'

'Luckily you don't have to,' said Amina tartly.

'But I would. I wouldn't sit about watching daytime TV, I'd be queuing at the supermarket for a job.'

'And if there were no jobs?' queried Jack.

'There are always jobs somewhere.' Inaya was fiercely angry. 'I'd scrub floors.'

'Yes, yes,' said Amina, 'you'll do every scummy job on the list, especially when there's no chance you'll ever have to.'

'My daughters quarrel all the time,' said Mr Choudhury.

Amina and Inaya were glaring at each other across the table. Jack had warmed to Amina and thought Inaya somewhat naive.

They'd made quite a hole in the food. Jack was feeling heavy and wondered whether they'd ever get outside. Get some space between people, talk stars and not property values. Though Jan had shown her colours. A free house dropped in her lap but she was quick enough to go on about benefit scroungers. He hadn't entered the fray, or barely. He had customers round here and couldn't be seen as a raving red.

'Let's set the telescopes up,' said Mr Choudhury. 'Then we'll come back for a quick coffee. And have everyone out to see the stars.'

Jan, Jack and Mr Choudhury rose.

Mia said hurriedly, 'I'll help Dad.' And got up too.

The four went into the conservatory where they had

their telescopes. Mr Choudhury opened the door to the patio, and they took their instruments outside. The night was on the far edge of twilight, the houses and trees blackening, the glow of sunset all but gone.

Chapter 12

There was a half moon, quite high in the sky. Jack suggested they should each go for it, then they could compare the performance of the telescopes. It was an easy one. No searching challenge, as the moon was there for all to see. Not like a nebula that was beyond the naked eye and had to be found in the darkness. Unless you set your goto on to it, not that that always worked; it would depend how well you'd aligned your instrument.

Light pollution was a big factor in any city. The best you could do was get away from lighted areas. They turned off the lights in the back of the house. Fortunately, the neighbours next door were out. Jan's house, two doors away, was in darkness. But the anarchists had a light on in the back.

'I could have a word with them,' said Jack. 'They know me.'

'Would you do that, Jack? It would make a difference,' said Mr Choudhury.

Jack took off his boots at the patio door, went through the house and put them back on again to go out the front door. The evening had picked up, now they were at their scopes. No talk of property prices and benefit scroungers. He'd left Mia to their telescope. She was quite in her element, focussing, changing eyepieces, chatting even.

He walked up the path of 72, the anarchists' house. There was a light on in the front. Surely they would turn off the back light.

He rang the bell. Waited a little while and rang again.

The anarchists were in the cellar at the front. They heard the bell ring. Then again and again. And they ignored it. Or rather, waited for silence. After a couple of minutes, they decided they could continue. It was Susie's turn.

A single bulb lit the low gloom. On a chair, against the bare bricks, was a large cardboard box that once held a fridge. The inside was packed with newspapers and discarded leaflets. On the side facing Susie had been drawn a crude picture of a policeman in an old fashioned high helmet holding a truncheon.

She pointed the gun, two arms extended, holding it as firmly as she could. She closed one eye, the other looking along the sight.

'Get on with it,' yelled Anton. 'Every cop in East London would have time to be here by now.'

She lowered the gun and glowered at him. 'What should I do then?'

'Just spin round and fire.' His hair was tied back in a tea towel.

'Right.' She turned her back on her target. Biting her lip, the gun low, almost at her knees, she took a deep breath. Then swivelled round and fired.

Susie jumped back in the recoil. The cellar shook in the bang, the acrid smell of detonator filling the space. Her ears rang as if punched.

Tosh was behind her, hands over his ears. She fell into him; he lifted her, while Anton went to the target. There he put his finger through the hole in the cardboard, about half an inch from the side of the policeman's helmet.

'My turn,' he said.

The three telescopes had centred on the crater Archimedes. The terminator, where light meets dark, cut it in two, showing the crater ridges in relief. As expected, Mr Choudhury's scope had the clearest image. Though it was the smallest too.

'You need a more powerful eyepiece, Mr Choudhury,' said Mia.

'I do, I do.'

'Though it's as clear as crystal,' she said.

Their own image was larger but fuzzier. Jan's better but smaller. The watchers went eagerly from eyepiece to eyepiece. The next challenge was Saturn.

Mr Choudhury pulled Jack aside as the others clustered round the telescopes.

'Can I have a word with you, Jack?'

'Of course.'

'Let's go inside.'

Jack glanced at Mia. She knew exactly what to do with their scope, and was pointing out Saturn in the sky to Amina and Inaya who were on their father's telescope. In appearance it was just a bright star, but Mia knew where it would be from looking at the astronomy magazine before they left.

Knowing she was fine, he left her and followed Mr Choudhury into the house.

The father of the house took Jack up the stairs to a medium-sized room, his office. Instead of turning on the top light, he turned on a standard lamp.

'Less spillage into the garden,' he said.

There was a desk along the garden window with a laptop on it along with various papers. To one side on an alcove shelf was a printer. There were books in the other alcoves in custom made shelves. Most in English, but he noted a couple of shelves with Urdu books. Or rather, he thought they were Urdu.

There was a dark leather armchair and a matching two-person sofa in the other half of the room. Mr Choudhury took the sofa and invited Jack to take the armchair.

'Your daughter knows her astronomy,' he said once they were comfortable.

'She reads my magazines,' he said. 'And we go out together with my telescope regularly.'

69

'Very commendable.'

Jack was aware that Mr Choudhury hadn't brought him up to his office to talk about telescopes. He noted the man's fingers playing on the arm of the sofa. He was biting his other knuckle.

'I'm in trouble, Jack.'

'I'm sorry to hear it.'

Mr Choudhury sighed. 'Overstretched. Greedy. The capitalist's curse. It's never enough.'

'I hope you can bear it,' said Jack. There was nothing he could say but platitudes in view of the vagueness.

Mr Choudhury was quiet for perhaps half a minute, his head shaking, sighing. Jack suspected he was battling how much to tell.

He said, 'I've got to sell the house.'

And looked at Jack to gauge his reaction. Jack couldn't take the intensity and turned away.

'Really, that bad?' he said.

'More than that bad.' He slapped the sofa cushion beside him. 'I've been an absolute fool. I own a sari-cum-women's clothing shop on Green Street. Not one of the big ones, but medium. It made us a comfortable living. With some help from my father I was able to buy this house twenty years ago. Five years ago, I saw an opportunity. Someone was selling five shops. A fire sale. I double mortgaged, scraped every penny I could from Peter and Paul. What a crazy fool, I tell you! So much money I had to push into fittings and stock... For a few years it looked fine. And then the market crashed...' His hands flew up in the air. 'And, I tell you, Jack. It's one big mess.'

'You've really got to sell this house?'

'No choice. I owe half a million, give or take, which I have to pay off in the next few months, or lose everything. My accountant says all I can do is sell the house. Pay my debts. Then I can just about keep my original shop, Allah be praised. And that leaves me a hundred thou or so for the down-payment on a smaller house somewhere.'

Jack looked about the room. At the bookshelves and armchairs. Twenty years of ownership, the family house. The carpets, the furniture, the curtains, the smell of the place, their movement freely round it. They'd made it theirs.

'I don't know what to do,' sighed Mr Choudhury.

'Do your wife and daughters know?'

He shook his head. 'No. I haven't told them.' He closed his eyes. His face was drawn, he pressed his plexus. 'It's shame. You see, relatives come here. They'll all be coming for Inaya's wedding in two weeks. They say what a wonderful house you have, Aklis.' He stretched his arms around. 'It is the measure of my success in the world. My castle in Forest Gate.'

'And there's no choice but sell?' said Jack. He realised he was repeating himself, but what else could he say?

'I am mortgaged to the hilt. And I've a big debt to pay. Or else.'

Jack was unable to come up with anything useful. There was enormity here, a tragedy. He had no money to offer. Some sympathy, sure, but zero advice.

'Why have you told me?' he said.

Mr Choudhury turned over his empty hands. 'Who else could I tell?' His shoulders were hunched. 'You don't move in my circles. You won't be talking to my relatives. You won't gossip at the mosque. My shame is safe with you.'

Jack felt the enormity. Here was a secret, bound to come out in time, but not from him.

'I shan't tell anyone,' he said. 'I can see it's been a trial for you to speak at all.'

'Oh, you don't know the half of it, Jack. It is such a comedown. I imagine all the talk among the relatives. Some of them will be secretly glad, I can tell you. Mr Bigshot has lost it all. Lock, stock and barrel.'

'You must tell the family.'

'I know. I know.' He closed his eyes, a blood vessel was beating under one eye. 'But how, when? What will they think of me? Their father. In my culture, I am their protector.'

'The sooner you tell them the better,' said Jack. 'They'll have to move with you to a smaller house. They'll have to deal with the relatives.'

Mr Choudhury moaned as if his stomach had split.

'You can't sell the house without telling them,' said Jack.

'No. I can't. But I don't know how to tell them.'

Jack suddenly had a thought. He had strayed to thinking of the house next door and it came to him.

'It's possible,' he said, 'you might be able to delay things. Stay here when you've sold up.'

'Please explain.'

He was staring at Jack as if he had an answer, a miracle. Which of course he hadn't. Simply an idea to hold off for a while.

'If Terry bought your house...' said Jack.

'Who is Terry?'

'Terry owns next door. The squatted house.'

'But I don't know Terry.'

'Neither do I,' said Jack. 'But Terry employs me. We know he can afford to buy one house and leave it empty. So perhaps a second...' Even as he spoke, Jack was unsure he should be offering this salvation, if even salvation it was. It involved him in someone's awful troubles. But it was too late now. 'Suppose,' he went on, 'I put it to him that he could buy your house, but instead of keeping it empty, you stay here.'

'For how long might that be?'

'I don't know. Next door has been empty nine months and he doesn't seem to be in any hurry to move in. I really don't know how long.' He stopped, he had no idea whether Terry would be at all interested. Who on earth was Terry? Mr Choudhury was watching him, wiping his face, struggling with money and months.

'The house goes in the end,' said Jack. 'It just wouldn't be so sudden. You would have somewhere to live while you were looking for a new house. You could adjust to the new circumstances.'

Boy, he sounded like a social worker. Alison was better at this stuff, but then she was a Head and dealt with it every day.

'Yes, yes,' said Mr Choudhury, vigorously nodding. 'That might be the best of a bad deal. Time, and no panic. I'd be grateful if you would see if it's possible. What sort of deal do you think he might offer?'

'I don't know,' said Jack. 'All I can do is sound him out.'

They sat in silence. Jack knew the house was part of Choudhury's identity. His piece of earth. His place in the extended family. A castle for his family, in money and bricks. He had gambled with it, and lost. He was ashamed of the betrayal, panicking over loss of face.

'I think we'd best join the others,' said Mr Choudhury wearily. 'They'll be wondering what we are up to. But please, keep all this to yourself.'

Jack promised again. And they went back to the telescope party.

Chapter 13

Mia had taken charge while Jack was out. After a view of Saturn, she returned to the moon, always her favourite. She trailed the craters and seas, at the same time helping the others. Jan was trying to capture the nebula in Orion's dagger, but it was already low in the sky and becoming smothered in the pollution glow of the horizon. Mr Choudhury came out with Jack, leaving his bad humour behind. He took over his telescope and delighted in the Pleiades in the constellation of Taurus, asking everyone to come see. His involvement in the here and now, catching the jewelled star cluster, made his earlier conversation with Jack seem an impossibility. But Jack could see the desperate busyness. Up there, way up, come see. Anywhere but down here, where he lived.

Back home close to eleven, Mia was still excited by the sights of the night and the attention she'd received. She'd been praised to the hilt as she went from scope to scope, working on the instruments and expounding on the sights they showed. She could easily have stayed up another hour or two, but Jack knew she'd regret it in the morning.

'Straight to bed,' said Jack. 'Your mother'd kill me if she knew you were up this late.'

'It's education,' she said dismissively. 'And I don't need much sleep.'

The telephone rang. Jack picked it up.

'Hello.'

'Hello, Jack.'

Jack put a finger to his lips and mouthed 'your mother' to Mia.

'How was your house hunting?' he said.

'Interesting. Is Mia in bed?'

'She's been in bed for over an hour.'

His daughter smirked. Jack rolled his eyes at his lie.

'Good. Has she done her homework?'

'Homework all done. Are you going to take the place?' He was desperate to get off talking about Mia. And wished she would leave the room, but without banging the door.

'I'm thinking of making an offer on it,' said Alison. 'They want 480 thou, I could try 460. Though it's all funny money. It exhausts me to think about such big numbers. It's a nice house though. Three bedrooms. A long garden down to the railway. I don't mind trains. They're quite comforting.'

'You'd better stick around here for a while,' said Jack. 'Our daughter is fed up with moving.'

'What did she say?'

'She says she was just making friends in Brighton and you upped sticks again.'

'I'd better stay put then,' said Alison. 'Though this school is not the best. But then it's up to me to make something of it.'

'Before you move again.'

'I never said that.'

Jack didn't want a row last thing at night. It was too easy to start sniping.

'It'll be good if you get the place,' he said placatingly. 'Less hassle for all of us, if you live nearby.'

'You've convinced me, Jack. I'll make an offer in the morning. Goodnight.'

She rang off. Jack was grateful to get off without an argument and without Mia being heard by Alison, for she'd stayed to listen.

'So she likes the house?' enquired Mia.

'She's going to put an offer in.'

'Be good to get out of that poky flat.'

'You'll be able to walk to school. And I'm only ten minutes away.'

'Not sure whether that's good or bad.' And she went to the bathroom.

Mia might be wide awake but he was weary himself. It had been a long day. Dealing with the squatters, the Jan interlude, and it had been an eventful evening. Mia had enjoyed herself which was great, but the private conversation with Mr Choudhury... The big house that had to be sold. The women of the house had been happy and enthusiastic watchers of the skies. Mrs Choudhury had brought them all out hot chocolate and biscuits. Laughter and squeals of joy... All unaware.

It had to be told. Mr Choudhury said there was no other way but sell the house. It made him think of his own shame in his alcoholic days. Drink the answer, drink the problem. Alison had kicked him out. Dreadful time. He shuddered at the memory. On the streets. How could people living in those big houses know anything about homelessness, living on benefits? Jan's cheap jibe surprised him. Kick the poor. Is that a way of congratulating yourself? Mrs Choudhury, she was on about scroungers too. She was going to be hit so hard very soon. Would they row? Or would she lie in bed sullen? Don't touch me. He remembered that himself. Alison's disgust.

He suspected that Amina would be more forgiving than Inaya. But Inaya was getting married, presumably going off to live somewhere else. Or was she? In this housing climate, the married couple might be staying at Mum and Dad's for a while. Not long, if that was the plan.

He must contact Terry. There was a chance a sale to him would give the Choudhurys some breathing space.

And that reminded Jack of the estimate he'd sent earlier in the evening. He turned on his computer. As he waited for the machine to warm up, he couldn't help thinking of the telescope party. The colourful saris, the cries of delight at the rings of Saturn, so assured of their place...

There was an email from Terry. Jack's estimate had been accepted and half the money put into his bank account. That meant work tomorrow, with a new intern. If the anarchists agreed to her presence.

Let tomorrow deal with that. But he sent a quick email to Jan, telling her the estimate had been accepted and asking if she was ready to start work in the morning.

That night, Aklis Choudhury tossed and turned in bed. His wife asked if anything was wrong. He said he'd eaten too much, don't worry. He forced himself to lie still. And she was soon asleep. He was tired but sleep was out for him, his head was too electric. He touched his wife on the shoulder; would she forgive him? His daughters. Oh, the shame. He arose; it was twenty past three, so much night left. He put on his dressing gown, the house had long cooled down. Should he have said so much to the builder? Did it matter? Likely not. Aklis didn't know him, he was just a man with a telescope. A nice enough chap, and he had an idea that might be helpful. At the extreme end of helpful. Once the house was sold. And that was unbearable.

He padded down the stairs to the kitchen. And looked in the fridge. There was a lot of food, leftovers from the meal and plenty else, but nothing he fancied. He stood gazing at the shelves for a minute or two before closing up. He was hungry, he wasn't hungry. He opened the fridge again. Nothing in there he fancied.

For half an hour tonight he'd been at peace. Not at dinner. That had been hell, too much a reminder of what he had to lose. His family round the table, guests. Here, in the house they'd been creating for twenty years. With the bomb about to fall... No. His joy had been the Pleiades. The glowing stars in the blackness. His delight as he brought the vision into sharpness, as if he possessed it.

It was not his. It was Allah's. All Allah's. Aklis's stupidity was his pride. His downfall.

He went into his office, lay out on to the sofa. And wept.

Chapter 14

It was an effort getting Mia up and out in the morning. She was sullen. She didn't want breakfast. He wasn't too worried about that as she'd had plenty to eat last night. Though Alison would go wild. Breakfast, for Mia at least, was a religion for her. Though he'd seen Alison herself leave the house with just a rushed cup of coffee.

Mia complained about having to put the same clothes on that she'd worn yesterday.

'We could have gone to the laundrette last night,' he said in annoyance, 'or to the star party.'

'Get a washing machine,' she spat. 'I don't know anyone else who hasn't got one.'

'Oh, you sound just like your mother.'

'She isn't always wrong, you know.'

He didn't want this first thing in the morning. But Mia was right. He could wear dirty clothes to work. Who knew or cared for a builder? But his daughter... He really should get a washing machine. It would have to be a washer-dryer as he had nowhere to dry clothes. Five hundred quid cash, or pay off forever. The van MOT was coming up, and he had to keep cash in hand in order to take on bigger jobs. Cash flow, the scourge of the self employed.

'I'll get a washing machine,' he said wearily.

'You said that two months ago.'

'Did I?'

'Yes.'

He might've done. A washing machine just wasn't that high on his priorities. But it was false economy not getting one. A few weeks back, with a date on, he'd had to go out and buy a shirt, underwear and socks. Not that she'd been worth it. But he shouldn't be buying new clothes with a heap of laundry overfilling the basket, including some of Mia's.

Being organised at work was as much as he could manage. All this laundry and cooking and cleaning... God save him. He wasn't born for it. He needed a robot, but while he waited for technology to catch up, he really should get a washing machine. This weekend. He could plumb it in himself.

In the meantime, he recalled they did a service wash at the launderette on Woodgrange. He filled a black bag with dirty washing, his and Mia's. He'd drop it in on the way to work, pick it up on the way home.

'I need money for lunch.'

Mia held her hand out. Alison would have made her sandwiches. Healthy options. Jack searched his pockets. He had one pound fifty in change.

'I can't get anything with that.'

He took out his wallet. He had a twenty pound note and nothing else. What could he do? Be more organised, but in default of that – he handed over the bank note.

'You can have a fiver,' he said. 'I expect the rest back.'

'What about some spending money?'

'Alright, a tenner. But that's it.'

He packed her off. And sat down with relief to finish his coffee. It was hard enough getting himself up and out in the morning. He had to admit though that if he hadn't taken Mia to the telescope party last night and stayed so late, she wouldn't be so tired, as the Alison-in-his-head told him. All his fault.

The odd late night wouldn't matter. Surely?

Jack was about to leave when he remembered Terry. He turned his computer on. While it was warming up, he put his tool box and bag of washing by the door to pick up as he left. Back at the computer, he noted an email from Aklis Choudhury had come in. Sent at four ten in the morning.

Great telescope session last night, Jack. Very impressed with your knowledgeable daughter. A credit to you. Thank you for listening to my troubles. I'd be grateful if you would contact the owner of 72, and see if he'll accept a deal for our place which allows us to stay for the time being. I have an idea of my own but not a great deal of confidence in it. Amina says you agreed to repair the patio. I'd be grateful if you could do the cheap option before Inaya's wedding. Thank you for everything.

Aklis

After reading it, Jack thought for a moment what to do. There was patio work needed at the squatters' place too. He could combine the jobs; get the sand and slabs delivered for both houses. Save money and time. Jack made a note in his workbook.

He replied to Aklis thanking him for last night's stargazing party and told him that he would do his patio work as soon as possible. Then he emailed Terry with the careful enquiry about whether Terry might want to buy the Choudhury house. And then left. As he drove, he thought about ordering the paving stones and other materials later today. Traffic was heavy on Woodgrange; he'd hit the school run and rush hour. A cyclist pulled across him just as he was pulling out of Earlham Grove. He braked sharply. Didn't she want to live? No helmet. Traffic was hooting at Jack as he was blocking the road. He turned into the stream of traffic and took the first left into Claremont. The road was quiet and he began to breathe freely. How easy it would have been to have killed that cyclist. A split second. Mia wanted to cycle to school. Alison wouldn't let her. Not on these roads. A cyclist has no protection.

He parked outside Jan's. As he got his toolbox out of the back of the van, he saw the black bag of washing he should have dropped in at the launderette.

'Hell. That's all I need.'

Jan was awaiting him in green overalls, a little paint

splattered but clean, hair in a work-a-day ponytail.

'Coffee?'

He hesitated at the door.

'What's up?' she said.

'I really should go to the laundrette,' he said. 'I've a bag of dirty washing in the back of the van. And no clean clothes. I had to send Mia to school in yesterday's gear.'

'Bring it in,' she said. 'Do it in my machine.'

'You sure?'

She gave him a bright smile which cheered him immensely. 'It's not doing anything now.'

He went back to the van and brought the black bag into the house. She led him out to her laundry room. The room was the size of his kitchen, with shelves on one wall with neat stacks of towels and sheets. Much more space than Jan could use.

'It's immense,' he said, on seeing her silver machine.

'It embarrasses me sometimes,' she said, 'when I've only a small wash. I inherited it. My grandmother towards the end was incontinent and had a live-in carer.'

'I must get a washing machine,' said Jack as he pushed the dirty washing into the machine.

'Why haven't you?'

'You get used to not having one.'

'You get used to having one,' she said.

The machine was set going and they adjourned to the kitchen for coffee.

'I'd have liked to have talked to you last night,' she said. She had light make-up on, not quite right for a builder's mate. 'Too many people about. Though I did enjoy it. First time I've had my telescope out in a year. Your daughter was great.'

'She loved it,' said Jack. 'But she's a wreck this morning.'

'She'll recover,' said Jan dismissively. 'Pity you couldn't come over last night. Is Mia with you tonight?'

'No.'

'Come for dinner.'

'I'll forget how to cook at this rate.' He laughed. 'Though that won't take long. Love to come.' He caught sight of the shoes she was wearing. 'Trainers are no good. Have you got any boots?'

'I've some leather walking boots.'

'Put them on. There's more accidents in the building trade than any other sector.'

'OK, boss.' She saluted.

He noted her clean white hands, the nails so clean, so beautifully filed, and wondered how long she'd last. And whether it'd be a chore telling her which end of a hammer was which.

'They might not let you in next door,' he said. 'It was hard enough me persuading them yesterday.'

'We can but try,' she said with a shrug. 'Just go in with confidence.'

They set off. It was odd to have a mate, a female one especially. And Jan really wasn't convincing as a builder. At one point as she'd been making the coffee, he had been tempted to suggest they go upstairs, to look at her telescope. He didn't doubt she would have agreed. But money to be earned, washing machines to be paid for... And the moment passed.

The sun was shining as they came out on to the street. Jack thought they should do the roof work today, to take advantage of the fine weather. Could be pouring tomorrow. The ladders were in the back garden on the patio, where he'd left them yesterday.

He rang the bell of 72. Jan crossed the fingers of both hands as they waited. Jack wondered who might open the door. Anyone but Anton.

Susie opened up. It was obvious she'd just woken up. Her face pale and sleep-worn, her hair mussed up. Her lips pursed as she noted them.

'Two of you?' she said with evident annoyance.

'I need a mate for the roof work,' said Jack.

She shook her head. 'We never agreed on two. No way.' She was holding the door, which she'd only opened about a foot. She called into the house. 'Tosh – come out here.' She turned back to them. 'I mean come on, Jack. This is just a liberty.'

He noted she too was wearing yesterday's clothes with added smears of printer's ink.

Jan said, 'I won't be any trouble. I don't care who lives here.'

Tosh had come to the door which opened wider.

'Hello, Jack,' he said, still doing up the buttons of his shirt. 'Who's she?'

'My mate for today,' he said.

Tosh grinned. 'No way, Jack. One was all the collective agreed to. You can't sneak her in.'

'Look at her hands,' exclaimed Susie. 'She's no builder. Never done a day's manual work in her life.'

'You a cop?' said Tosh to Jan.

'Of course I'm not,' countered Jan. 'Do I look like a cop? I live next door. There.' She pointed to her house. 'I'm a writer.'

'A two a penny wordsmith!' declared Susie. 'Come to write us up for the Daily Mail?'

'I write children's books,' said Jan soothingly.

'Which ones?' snapped Tosh.

Jan sighed. 'I am the author and illustrator of the Space Cat series.'

'You?' said Susie. 'You write *Mimi the Space Cat*?'

'I do,' she said. 'I've done fifteen...'

'I love *Mimi the Space Cat*!' exclaimed Susie, throwing her arms wide.

Tosh tapped Susie on the shoulder. 'Hang about. Save the enthusiasm. Let's check this out.' He turned to Jan. 'You say you do the Space Cat books?'

'I do. I'm Jan Fletcher.'

'I sort of remember them,' said Tosh. 'Ask her something about them, Susie?'

Susie scratched her cheek for a few seconds, then said 'How do they get off the beautiful planet?'

'Right. That should tell us whether you're a cop or not,' said Tosh. 'How do they get off the beautiful planet?'

Jan bit her thumb. 'That's one of the earlier ones. Ten years ago or more. Way back. Let me think. Oh yes, I remember. Obo the robot waits until Jake and Mimi fall asleep, then ties them up and carries them back to the spaceship.'

'Is that right?' said Tosh.

'It is,' said Susie, obviously unsure how to progress.

'Would you like to come next door?' said Jan. 'I'll prove to you who I am.'

Susie looked to Tosh who shrugged. 'Why not?'

'Where's Anton?' said Jack.

'Out,' said Tosh.

He offered no further details and Jack didn't press him. Jan led them next door. As they strolled, she was telling them about the next series she was planning, about three builders, and she wanted to do some practical research. Next door was so convenient for her.

She took them into her workroom and showed them the sketches she was doing for the building books, the animals, the tools. Then took a large folder off a shelf which she laid out on the floor.

'This is what I take into schools,' she said. 'To show the kids how a picture book is put together. First I write the story.' She showed the typed story of *Stranded in Space*. 'It's about 850 words. Once I've got the story and my editor is happy with it, I split the words into pages, some double spreads. Then I do a storyboard.'

She took out two A1 sheets and spread them on the

carpet. Each contained about a dozen pencil sketches for the story, following on from each other, with the words underneath.

'I have to get this right before I can begin doing the finished pictures,' she went on, 'or I waste so much time. So there's trial and error, going backwards and forwards, lots of screwed up sheets... Then, when I've got it, I start at the beginning and do the pictures one at a time. I spend more time on the first few as I've got to get the colours and background right.'

From the folder, she took out a couple of A3 coloured pictures from the story.

'These are the finished pictures. Some illustrators these days work totally on computer, but I went to art school and prefer to paint them. Old fashioned, I suppose. Takes me three months to do the lot, then I take them in to the publishers and they scan them into their computer, get them to size and assemble the artwork for printing.'

Tosh and Susie were captivated.

'These are so good,' said Susie, almost drooling.

'I wish I'd gone to art school. Would have been more useful than medieval history,' said Tosh. 'I've been having a go at an anarchist comic.'

'I've done two comic novels myself,' Jan said. 'I'd be happy to talk about the ideas you've got. Why don't you show me your draft?'

'That'd be good. Yeh, I will.'

She offered them coffee and toast, which they eagerly accepted. In the kitchen, while she made the beverages and toast, she told them about her thoughts for the new series. Jack was simply background; it was Jan's bat, Jan's ball and Jan's pitch. She was certainly impressive on her home ground. Watching her operate, he'd noted that once they'd begun to look at her pictures, she had them. The marmalade toast and coffee were hardly needed.

Chapter 15

They began upstairs where a bedroom door was almost off. It had ripped away a long peel of door jamb and was barely hanging on a couple of screws from one hinge. Jack put wedges under the door to support it while he carefully removed the screws.

'A door is quite a weight,' he told Jan. 'If it falls, you could do your hands in or your back.'

Jan was watching, taking photos with a small camera from time to time. Once the door was off, Jack measured up and sent off Jan with his keys to get timber from his van. The hinges were fine, the door was sound. He should have asked her to bring the broom, pan and brush. Never mind, it would keep her busy, running and fetching. He sorted out screws from his toolbox.

Jan selected a length of 4 by 2 from the van. It was slightly oversize; Jack had said she wouldn't find an exact piece. She locked up the van and balanced the timber on her shoulder, feeling like a real builder, trying no hands as she walked up the path.

'Who the hell are you?' came a yell from behind.

She turned, just managing to stop the timber falling, and saw a short, scruffy young man coming up the path behind her. His hair was to his shoulders, his face dark, quite dirty.

'I'm working with the builder,' she said, holding the timber upright to support her professional claim.

'No, you're not!'

The young man strode past her into the house.

'Who let that tart in!' he yelled.

He went into a side room, slamming the door after him. Other voices joined his. That must be Anton, she thought, as

87

she picked up the timber and put it over her shoulder. The awkward one according to Jack. On the button.

Susie and Tosh were cleaning the platen on the offset litho when Anton stormed in.

'What the hell's that woman doing here!'

'Helping Jack,' said Susie calmly.

Anton threw his arms in the air. 'I knew this would happen. Let one in and we'd have an army in...' He turned on them, his fingers clawing the air, as if to tear their skin. 'We have a job on tomorrow. I've just picked up the car. And you fill up the place with flaming builders. What pair of babes in arms am I working with?'

'She lives next door, Anton,' said Tosh, trying to calm him down. 'She's harmless.'

'I don't give a damn where she lives.' He slapped his hands to his head. 'The more people coming and going, the more likely someone is going to spot something going on. How did I get lumbered with such a pair of amateurs!'

'Cool it, Anton,' said Susie. 'Just because you've done time, doesn't make you our boss.'

Anton was striding about the room, eyes raised, hands clumped to his head.

'Tomorrow we'll have twenty thousand quid...' He pointed out of the room. 'Will that tart be here?'

'There aren't any tarts here,' exclaimed Susie, hands on hips. 'Unless you're one.'

'She's gotta be out,' hissed Anton. 'The two of them. Out of here.'

'Take it easy, Anton,' said Tosh with a sigh. 'You come in screaming and yelling like a banshee. You just put our backs up. Stay cool.'

'Tomorrow's job is not for a pair of fluffies. It's gotta be smooth. It's gotta be calculated.'

'Like you're doing now?' interjected Susie.

'Like I would be, if there were just three of us in this house. She's gotta go. And throw Jack of All Trades out with her.'

'Shall we vote on it?' said Tosh.

'Couples!' He threw his hands up. 'How did I get lumbered with you schoolkids!'

He strode out of the print room, slamming the door behind him, shaking the house.

Jack and Jan could hear the row below, but not the words of it. Jack was sawing the 4 by 2 to size. He had it on the only chair in the house.

'Anton clearly doesn't want me here,' said Jan quietly, sitting on the hall carpet. 'Not one tiny bit.'

'I only got in after a bribe,' said Jack, his eyes on the pencil line and the saw.

'He's got one hell of a temper,' mused Jan. 'Like my ex-husband.'

'You don't sound too fond of him...' The end of the timber came off into his hand.

'He was charming,' she said. 'Good looking. But also a possessive, insecure, pile of steaming manure. The main reason I'm here and not in Maldon.'

'Is he in your house there?'

'He most certainly isn't. I got rid of him in the end. The house is now let to a lecturer at the University of Essex and his family. But my ex-husband is around the town. Too much around for me.'

Chapter 16

Aklis Choudhury was huddled in a corner of his sofa, knees clutched to his chest, in his upstairs office. He was still in his pyjamas and dressing gown. On the floor were screwed up pieces of paper, with figures and crossings-out. His face was drawn, heavy with weariness, the air stale in the closed room. The sun was coming in his window over the roofs at the end of his garden. If he had the energy, he'd draw the curtain. The night had dragged, the day was dragging. The Green Street shop would have to run without him today. What did it matter, the one shop left of the six? The original. What did anything matter? He was nobody, less than nobody. Everything was lost. He'd blow his brains out, jump from a tall building, if it wasn't so much effort.

He should run off. Pack a bag, grab every penny he could, fly away and disappear in the streets of Lahore. There he could beg on the streets, ask for alms from the mosque, a complete unknown. Here, in Forest Gate, he'd spent his whole adult life keeping up appearances. A model father and husband, the epitome of the self-made man, a well-read pillar of the community. Look up to him and emulate. His table full, charities knew where to come, he was on the board of the Chamber of Commerce.

He would send in a letter of resignation to them all. I, Aklis Choudhury, resign from the middle class. I resign as father, husband, homeowner. I resign from every board and committee. Thank you for your past support.

Tears were welling again. Useless. Womanly. He couldn't even be a man. There had to be an end to it. A bridge, a railway line, never mind the Koran. Jump. He had sins in plenty. Pride, stupidity.

There was a knock on his door. He closed his eyes as if to shut out the sound.

'Go away.'

There was another knock.

'I said go away.'

The door opened. His wife was at the threshold with a tray holding a cup of tea and a plate of biscuits. She was in yellow and red salwar kameez, not wearing a hijab as she was indoors with only her husband. Her hair was below her shoulders, the darkest of browns, almost black, with a few streaks of grey.

'I wondered if you were ill,' she said.

'It's true,' he said. 'I'm not well.'

'Should you go to the doctor?' she asked.

He sighed. 'It's not that sort of unwellness, Badra.'

'I know you didn't sleep,' she said, coming into the room. 'Several times in the night, I woke up and you weren't there. Do you want this tea?'

'Yes, I'll have it.'

She placed it on the low glass-topped table beside the sofa. And sat on the arm of the armchair.

'I think you're depressed,' she said.

'I am.' He sat up and took up the tea cup, holding it in two hands like a life preserver. 'Very depressed.'

Neither spoke for a little while. He was drinking the tea, it was sugared, a little energy on an empty morning.

'My mother would say,' she said, 'when I was unhappy, that it must be love or it must be money.'

'I would never argue with your mother,' he said, with the shadow of a grin, that died at once.

'So who are you in love with?'

'My wife and my daughters.'

'Then it's money,' she said.

He did not reply. And so she knew what she had suspected. Hints had been dropped by friends and acquaintances when she was out shopping or popping in for her community work.

'I know the other five shops have not been doing well,' she said.

'A stupid purchase,' he said with a wave of his hand. 'Down the tubes.'

'And our Green Street shop?'

'I hope we can keep it.'

She was close, too close to what she feared. She hesitated asking the big question, but it could not be avoided.

'And the house?'

He didn't reply. Not looking at her, but into the cup where bits of biscuits floated. He's so scruffy, she thought. Like a man who has been ill for weeks, living on his own. And perhaps he had been.

'We will lose the house?' she queried.

He nodded. And he was crying, dropping the cup, the warm tea spilling on his feet and pyjama bottoms. She stooped and picked up the cup and put it on the table. And then sat next to him. She too wanted to weep, but it wouldn't do to have the two of them weeping. This was not a funeral. She always kept out of his business affairs. Her zone was house and family. And now they had crashed together, like an asteroid smashing into a planet.

She felt weak and hollowed, taking his hand, more in fear than support. She was about to hear what she didn't want to know. When the man of the family ceased to be the man. Tears came, she could not stop them, at the thought of the removal lorry, all their life here thrown in, and ferried heaven knows where. At the gossip and the pity of their relatives.

'Tell me everything,' she said. 'We have Amina and Inaya to consider. There might yet be something we can do.'

PART THREE:
UP ON THE ROOF

Chapter 17

Jack was re-hanging the door, putting the screws in the hinges, Jan was sweeping up sawdust with a brush and dustpan, the ponytail patting her neck, when Anton came up the stairs, stomping up to let them know he was coming, that he disapproved, and they could not escape him.

Once at the top of the stairs, he turned to face them hissing, walking slowly towards them.

'Here it comes,' whispered Jack. 'Say nothing out of order.'

She nodded as Anton approached, continuing to clear up as Jack screwed in the final screws in the top hinge. Anton had reached them, and stood watching them work as if they were a film, mouth slightly open, daring them to react.

'Do you want something, Anton?' said Jan pleasantly.

'You out.'

He was almost over her. Jack was afraid he might hit her, she was on her knees, she would be unable to evade a blow to her neck or a boot in her face.

'I'm not a spy,' she said, looking up at him, holding the pan and brush as an ineffectual shield. 'It's not my business who lives here.'

'Hands like that, you've never done a day's work in your life.'

She rolled her eyes, Jack bit his lip. Anton's temper might be laughable, but it wouldn't do to taunt him. Though being here at all was a taunt, having brought in Jan... A challenge too far. Anton was bound to do something. He couldn't walk away. Manly stupidity demanded that he act.

Anton picked up an offcut. He tried it in one hand then the other as if assessing it for weight and balance. Jack eyed his hammer, considering whether to go for it.

'We don't want any trouble, Anton,' he said.

'Then leave before you get it.'

Anton turned and strode swiftly away, his back bent, holding the offcut like the classic caveman. At the top of the stairs, he swivelled and hurled the timber. They both ducked as it flew over their heads and smashed into the wall behind them. When they looked again, he was out of sight, clumping down the stairs.

'We need to keep well out of his way,' said Jack. 'And hope he gets used to us.

In a few minutes, they'd completed the door repair. Making as little sound as possible, they came down the stairs. The printer was whirring in the print room, a smell of oil and ink flowing from the open door. Jack and Jan continued along the hallway and went out the back door to the patio.

The sun was bright in an almost clear sky. Daffodils were waving in the breeze, tulip buds fattening. Jack wondered whether Terry had a gardener as the grass needed a cut. Not his problem. It was good to get out of that stuffy house.

Jack began to pick up his extension ladder, when Jan stopped him.

'Excuse me, Boss. But I don't get these ladders. How do they work?'

He screwed up his face. Ladders were obvious. 'What don't you get?'

'This double one is two,' she said. 'Excuse my ignorance.'

He understood. It was a Mia question. The obvious isn't always so obvious.

'This is a double extension ladder,' he said, 'One length goes above the other, giving us a long ladder that will get us to the top of the house.'

'I've seen window cleaners with them,' she said.

'Except window cleaners don't work on roofs. The ladder

gets us there, but it mustn't be resting on the guttering. The gutter would collapse and anyone on the ladder could come crashing down. So we have this piece, a stand-off.' He picked up an almost triangular frame; its apex about the size of a ladder rung. 'The small side attaches to a top rung of the ladder with these wing nuts,' he went on. 'The long side presses against the wall. It holds the ladder off the guttering and keeps it steady at the top. You with me?'

'Makes sense. How does the roof ladder work? It's got wheels and hooks.'

'You should be paying me for this,' he said a little impatiently.

'I'm working for nothing, remember?'

'True. And two people with a ladder is safer. Sorry. Anton's put me in a mood.'

'I'll be more useful if I know what I'm doing.'

'Point taken,' he said. 'So the roof ladder. If you worked straight on the tiles of the roof, you'd probably break more tiles than you repaired and risk slipping off and breaking your neck in the bargain. So we use a roof ladder to work on the slope. It lies on the roof from the guttering to the ridge. It has these over-hooks on the end which go over the roof ridge to support it. Then you can work off the ladder in safety. You can almost walk up it or get down on all fours. When we want to move it along the roof, you sit on the ridge, detach the hooks, turn over the ladder, and it's got these wheels so we wheel it to its next position and attach the hooks over the ridge again. Get it?'

'I think so.'

'It'll make sense in practice. Let's get up there.'

Jack looked up to the eaves, estimating the height needed, then extended the double extension ladder.

'Another few rungs higher,' he said, pushing the top section over the guttering.

He let it out further until the ladder was a few rungs over

the gutter. Then, with Jan's assistance, he brought the ladder down and screwed on the stand-off. He put the ladder up again. This time, instead of resting against the gutter, the stand-off pressed on the wall below the guttering, holding the ladder firm against the brickwork. Jack pushed against the ladder with both hands and a foot on the lower rung, testing its rigidity.

'The foot has to be 1 in 4 out,' he said. 'What's that roof? 6 metres high, that's a metre and a half out. More or less.' He laid a sandbag by the foot of the ladder. 'That stops the foot slipping. Essential when I'm working on my own. It doesn't pay to rush ladders. I've seen a guy once climbing up a triple extension ladder with a full bucket of cement, and I'm thinking he only has to slip – and he's in a wheelchair for the rest of his life.'

'Thank you, boss,' she said with a mock salute. 'I've never been up a ladder higher than my step ladder at home.'

'Sorry I was impatient,' he said. 'I hate these jobs where they don't like you in the house. You feel the atmosphere coming off like smoke.'

'Let's not let him wind us up,' she said. 'Why don't I bring us out a thermos of coffee?'

'Great idea.'

Jan went off, climbing over the brick garden wall that separated her house from this. That way she'd avoid Anton in the print room. Jack put on his helmet and picked up the roof ladder. It wasn't heavy, being aluminium, but was a little cumbersome, and he set off climbing, one hand on the ladder, the other holding the roof ladder, taking it easy.

Once at the top, he pushed the roof ladder on to the roof itself and slid it up the tiles on its pair of front wheels, up to the ridge. Then he flipped it over, and the hooks went over the ridge. He pulled at the roof ladder, testing it for firmness. Fine.

Jack assessed the roof for repairs. Two tiles needed

replacing this side, another three had slipped, so just needed putting back into place. He'd found half a dozen spare tiles in the shed at the back of the garden, saving the chore and money of going off to buy them.

All set.

As he was climbing down, his phone rang. He wasn't going to answer it on a ladder, so continued to the bottom as it rang on. Once there, he took it out of his pocket.

Alison. What did she want now?

'Hello.'

'What the hell do you think you are doing, Jack Bell?'

'Fixing a roof,' he said.

'I've just had a phone call from Mia's school. She fell asleep in class. She told them she was up till half eleven. Is that so?'

'We went to a telescope party,' he said.

'Half eleven! She's twelve years old!'

'I didn't know it would be that late.'

Jan was climbing back over the garden wall with a small backpack over her shoulder.

'Can we talk about this some other time?' he said, suspecting they couldn't.

'They want me to go in and get her,' Alison went on.

'I'll get her,' said Jack.

'No, you won't. That's the last time she stays with you.'

The call rang off. Jack blew out his cheeks.

Jan was taking the thermos out of her bag and a packet of biscuits. 'Trouble?' she said.

'Mia fell asleep in class. Her mum's blaming me for keeping her up late.' He held up his hands. 'Guilty as charged, m'lud. She says that's the last time she stays with me.'

'Do you think so?'

'For a while. Till she's got a date. Or Mia gets at her non-stop.' He wriggled his neck to release tension. 'It's done with.

Let's have some coffee. Oh, she does annoy me. Though it's my fault. I admit it.'

'A storm in a teacup,' said Jan with a shrug, pouring out two cups of coffee. 'It's not as if Mia got run over. Not even a case of measles. Just a sleepy schoolgirl. The school overreacted. They should've put her in the sickbay for an hour.'

'That's schools for you,' he said. 'Open those biscuits. Forget my ex. Forget Anton and his tantrums.'

'Good for a plot though,' mused Jan. 'Angry householder raging at my builders. Should be able to use that.'

They drank and munched for ten minutes, sitting on a garden bench on the patio by a large container which had miniature daffodils and tulips in bud aching to burst.

'To work,' said Jack, standing up and brushing off crumbs. 'We'll begin with the broken tiles. You okay with heights?'

'I'm fine.'

'Then I'll go up with the tools and a bucket to take the broken tiles down in. When I call you, come up with one of those tiles.' He pointed out the heap. 'Don't forget your helmet. In fact, put it on now in case I drop something.'

Jan put on the yellow helmet, the end of her ponytail sticking out the back.

'Suits you,' he said.

He was tempted to kiss her, the yellow of the helmet so attractive with her blue eyes and freckled face. But instead slung a canvas bag of tools over one shoulder and began climbing the ladder. The bucket he carried over his wrist, so he had two hands on the ladder. Down below, she watched him climb, up the brickwork of the house, past the windows on ground and first floors, to the eaves.

At the top, Jack halted. He took an S-hook out of his bag, attached it to the top rung and hung the bucket from it. He climbed over the guttering and on to the roof ladder. It was sturdy, the slope fine, though he held the edges for security as he made his way up to a broken tile. There, he suspended his tool bag from another S-hook onto the roof ladder. He'd learnt to take care with tools on roofs; too easy for them to go clattering down to smash something or somebody.

The tile had a piece snapped off, probably in a storm. He put a couple of wedges under the two good tiles above, lifting them a couple of inches. Then with a trowel, he raised the broken tile so the nibs on the back lifted clear of the wooden batten. He then drew the tile out on the trowel, steadying it with his thumb as it came.

Jack put the trowel away in the bag, and climbed back down the roof ladder with the broken tile. He put it in the bucket hanging from his extension ladder.

He called down, 'Bring up a tile, Jan!'

She waved from the foot of the ladder, and began to climb. He watched her rising, the tile in one hand, steadily up the ladder, her yellow helmet like the nose of a slow rocket. The ladder bowed a little, but was firm at the stand-off and the foot. The sun had gone behind a cloud, and the temperature had dropped a few degrees.

Jan's head came over the guttering and then up a couple of rungs further.

'Your tile, boss.'

She handed over the red tile. It was a simple plain tile, not heavy. He took it from her and rested it on a rung of the roof ladder.

'Take the bucket down with the broken one and bring up another...' he began.

But Jan was yelling. 'The ladder!'

Her arms flailed for the briefest of instants, one hand gripping the guttering, the other managing to grab a rung of the roof ladder. The guttering was pulling away, her legs dangling in space. She let go of the gutter, hanging by one hand to a rung of the roof ladder, searching desperately with the other for a hold. Her helmet fell to the ground and bounced on the patio. Jack grabbed at the arm hanging from the roof ladder, her face in panic as she stared up at him, legs kicking in air, most of her body off the roof.

He leaned forward, as far as he dared, and drew her up the roof ladder, over the guttering, until she was able to grip the rungs with two hands. Jack took her shoulders and helped her upwards, until her feet had a footing. Only then did he release her. She lay face down, stretched out along the ladder, eyes closed, breathing heavily, Jack above, watching.

'You OK?'

She waved a hand as if to prove she were still alive. 'I think I am.' She was clutching the roof ladder like a infant her mother's breast. 'The ladder went from under me. I just grabbed out. The guttering pulled away like you said it would. Luckily, I grabbed a rung on the roof ladder.'

'The extension ladder was secure,' said Jack. 'I double checked. It can't have fallen by itself. Someone must've...'

'Anton!' she spat. 'It has to be. I only just got a hold,' she exclaimed. 'Oh Jack, if I'd been holding the bucket, I'd have been a goner.'

She was still face down, gasping as if rescued from drowning. Slowly, she turned on to her front, her eyes closed into the sun.

'No rush,' said Jack. 'Get your breath back.'

'The pig might've killed me.'

He was sure the double extension ladder up to the roof had been firm, had seen it as she was climbing. The stand-off had been secure on the wall, the sandbag holding the foot. There could be only one explanation; someone had pulled the ladder away.

She opened her eyes and held a hand out in front of her. 'Look. I'm trembling, I'm a jelly.'

'You did brilliantly,' he said, meaning it. He'd acted

quickly, but it would have been of no avail if Jan hadn't been quick herself. That was the way of it up top; if anything goes wrong, you have the briefest of moments to react.

The sun went into a cloud. Shadow covered the gardens.

'I'm not coming up here again,' she said. 'Sorry, Jack. Not with that maniac around.'

Jack took her hand and squeezed. She took it to her lips and kissed the back of his. For perhaps a minute, neither spoke. Jack was thinking how close death is. No matter how alive you are, it's always waiting.

'How we going to get down?' she said, releasing his hand.

Jack hadn't thought so far, his concern had been for her. But of course, there was a problem. The ladder was gone.

Jan sat up. 'I've my phone. We could call the fire brigade.'

'No need for that,' said Jack hurriedly, not wanting to look an idiot, a builder stuck up on a roof. 'There's that skylight.' He pointed it out. 'Over there. We go up to the ridge, slide ourselves along and move the roof ladder along with us, so we can get down to it. I've got some tools.' He indicated his bag. 'I can open the window one way or another.'

She looked up at the ridge, then across to the skylight.

'Another plot for a story,' she said with a half smile. 'I shall call it *Up on the Roof*. Anton is so helpful with my plots. I shall have to give him an acknowledgement.' She sighed, holding up a hand to stall him. 'Give me a minute, Jack. My heart's beating like a steam hammer.'

'Take your time,' he said. 'No rush.'

'My magnolia is in full bloom,' she said, pointing it out in her garden. 'And see my camellia, blood red flowers, always so early...' She turned to him, 'Pity we left the coffee and biscuits below.'

In a few minutes, Jan said she was OK. And they climbed the roof ladder up to the ridge. They sat astride it, a leg on either side, seeing the street as well as the back gardens. A woman with a pushchair looked casually up at them. Jack waved, she waved back. It had almost returned to a working day. He turned over the roof ladder until the top of it was resting on its wheels. He then bottomed himself along the ridge, heading to the place above the skylight, wheeling the roof ladder sideways with him. Jan came after, helping to steady the ladder as they traversed.

Jack stopped when the roof ladder ran down to the side of the skylight. He turned over the ladder and made sure the hooks were firmly over the ridge. Then, putting the bag of tools over his shoulder, he climbed down to the window. He had a screwdriver, a trowel and a hammer in his bag; not the best selection, but he'd manage one way or another. He ran his fingers round the window. It opened from inside; he could see the catch through the glass. He'd need a cold chisel to prise it open. Failing that, it was a brute hammer job. Smash the glass.

Pity. But in the scheme of things, a trifle.

Chapter 18

They went back to Jan's for lunch. Though Jan ate little. She was still shaky.

'That's my stint as a builder for today,' she said. 'Tomorrow morning, I'll come along, so long as there's no roof work.'

'Don't worry,' he said. 'Strictly ground level tomorrow. We can do the patio. In fact, I'll phone the supplier now.'

Jack phoned through his order for sand, mortar and paving stones, enough for both houses. And was told they'd come late afternoon.

He left Jan. She said she had some ideas that she'd like to sketch out, but would have a shower first. That would calm her down. He wasn't to worry. She was at home and had work to do.

Going back to the squatted house, Jack found the front door open. He went straight to the print room. Posters were shooting through the clattering machine, piling up on the platen. All three of the anarchists had black hands and smudges on their faces as if they were the team colours. Anton was crouched on the floor, cleaning a printing plate with a small brush and a saucer of solvent. The room was heavy with the fumes of ink and oil.

Jack put a hand on Anton's shoulder. Anton looked up at him.

'You might've killed her,' said Jack.

Anton screwed up his eyes and shrugged off Jack's hand. 'What are you talking about?'

'Taking away the ladder,' he said.

'What ladder, when?' said Anton, seemingly offended by the accusation.

'My ladder, out there, when Jan was up top,' said Jack precisely.

Anton turned to the others in exasperation and shouted above the racket, 'Have I been anywhere this morning?'

'No,' yelled Susie. 'Been here all the time.'

'All three of us,' shouted Tosh.

Group solidarity, thought Jack. The party line. He glared at them. What was the point of having a go at Anton? At any of them. They'd simply stick together and deny everything.

'Next time, I'll call the police,' he exclaimed.

And strode out of the room, realising almost at once it was a feeble threat. Next time? Was he expecting another assault? And then he'd call the cops, when he or Jan was lying dead on the deck.

Should he call them now? Nothing could be proved, but it would at least keep the police informed and make the anarchists wary. But all the fuss, all the time it would take... And he talked himself out of it.

He decided to go back on the roof and finish the work. The roof ladder was still up there. This time though, he wouldn't use his extension ladder but go out through the loft window. It was completely shattered as he'd hammered out all the glass. He would now be free to go in and out of through the bare window. Much safer than on a ladder, with Anton on the ground. Without a ladder on the ground, he'd be safe on the roof.

Jack carried his step ladder up the stairs to the bathroom. He pushed up the loft opening and went back down for the tiles needed for the roof repairs and carried them up to the loft. His tools were there already, left from when he and Jan had climbed in.

It was a fine afternoon, the sun staying out. Jack worked steadily. It was peaceful up high on his own, above the gardens and the street, knowing exactly what he had to do, and getting on with it. The only hassle was moving the roof ladder while sitting astride the ridge, a little undignified but lots safer than climbing up and down the ladder. He wondered whether Anton had spent his anger. If Jan had fallen and, most likely, been killed, the police would be here. Anton would be the prime suspect. Would his mates still give him an alibi?

It occurred to Jack that Anton's fingerprints would be on the ladder... The thought marinated as he worked, replacing the broken tiles and securing those that had shifted. Late afternoon, Jack went out to the back garden. The ladder was still resting against the wall of the house; he hadn't moved it since the assault. It had been drawn down a metre or so, just enough to pull away from Jan. Jack examined the side of the ladder, about shoulder height.

There were inky fingerprints on both sides.

Chapter 19

Amina was strolling back from school, coming past Forest Gate station. Outside was that odd circular redbrick kiosk. It had been a florist for a few years and now sold hot drinks and pancakes, though she never saw any customers. How long would it last before it was something else? The question she always wanted to ask, with the space so small, was what do you do about the toilet? Did the woman use the staff facilities in the station, as there were no public ones? Or what? Such trifling thoughts she had, as she came and went from school.

Today had been a little unsatisfactory. Janice, the other teaching assistant, a middle aged English woman, had left her to do most of the clearing up again. She didn't want to have a row with her, that would make it unpleasant for them both. But it wasn't fair. And Janice was always snapping at children. They were afraid of her. That wasn't the way, Amina knew. Kids don't learn anything if scared out of their wits.

Never mind, leave it behind, she was done for the day. Except these little things did annoy.

She was watching secondary schoolchildren streaming along the pavement in their various groups, yelling out to each other. There were so many schools round here, and all the children seemed to leave at once. They crowded the chicken shops. She grimaced at all that awful cheap, greasy food. Four chicken shops! No wonder children were fat these days.

She went past the church with the statue of the man stuck to the wall, fifteen feet up in the air, holding a book and bellowing at the street. Every day she looked up at him, and wondered what he might be yelling at the world: 'Leave the betting offices, leave the chicken shops, get down on your knees and beg for mercy before the world ends.'

They were so similar, Christianity and Islam, really. Like two football teams. You supported one or the other. Never both. That amused her, both had their club houses and team regalia. The boys in her class were all West Ham fans. Last term the class had gone to the stadium on a school visit and been shown around the stands, the changing room and the club museum. A good idea for the football club, capturing them young. Though the kids had loved it. Soon the team would be moving to the Olympic Stadium in Stratford, a pity really. Away from the hubbub of Green Street, out on its own, almost another country.

School was good for her, she knew. It broadened her horizons. Got her out of the house, made her think. She'd started work when she was eighteen, working in her father's shop. She hadn't liked it, feeling rather spied upon. And she never met any English people. It was better now she was a TA in a local school; her mother and father hadn't been so happy, but that really was the point. She wanted to be out of their sphere, have time to herself. And now she had plans to be a teacher; she'd sent for an application form for a college. She wouldn't tell her parents just yet, wait till she got accepted before she battled that one.

Amina passed the flats near the end of her road. Forest Point, the tower block, didn't look bad, but she'd never been inside. It was the low rise flats at the foot that dismayed her, so boxy and ugly. All those people on top of each other. She counted herself lucky to live in a big house, with plenty of space for all the family, not crushed in by neighbours, though she would like to see the squatted house next door properly inhabited by a family.

Jack was on the roof of the squatted house as she came by. He was on a roof ladder in his yellow helmet, out the

109

front. Though there wasn't a ladder to the roof. That puzzled her. How had he got up and down? Magnetic boots. She'd read the children a story about a boy who could walk up walls. Not so likely for Jack.

He gave her a wave, she gave him one back.

'I'll be doing your patio tomorrow,' he yelled.

'I'll make sure you get a cup of tea,' she called back.

'Don't forget the cake!'

She smiled and went up the path to 74. She opened the front door, and instantly her mother was there. She was wearing her best sari, the one she'd bought for Inaya's wedding. It was a deep purple with gold edging with a matching hijab.

'What's going on?' exclaimed Amina.

Her mother beamed at her, and said quietly, 'We have a most important visitor. Please be on best behaviour.'

'Who on earth is it?'

Amina had taken off her shoes and put them on the rack by the door. She put on her slippers.

'Come and meet him,' said her mother.

Amina was ushered into the front room.

There was her father in his suit in an armchair, looking cheerful, and a man she'd not seen before. Middle aged, almost bald, quite portly in a grey suit. He stood up from the other armchair as she came in.

'This is my daughter, Amina,' said Aklis. He too had risen.

'Pleased to meet you,' said the man in English. 'My name is Wasif Khan.'

'Pleased to meet you,' she said.

Amina sat down on the sofa. There was tea on the low table with biscuits and cake. She noted it was the best china, and wondered who Wasif Khan might be.

Her mother fussily passed the biscuits and cake. Mr Khan refused any, but Amina was peckish and took a piece of cake

110

and a plate. Her father and the man were talking business, something about leases and the different costs of material imported from Pakistan and from Bangladesh. She had nothing to say on this. She didn't own a shop and didn't buy material, having left shop life behind well over a year ago. Of course, her father was in that world and it seemed likely Mr Khan was too.

'And how was your day, dear?' said her mother.

She noticed that both her father and Mr Khan were looking at her. She wondered what they wanted her to say. What was so important?

'We did some very messy painting,' she said. 'And I took some of the children out one at a time for individual reading. Do you know that some children don't have a book in the house? And their parents never read to them, ever.'

'I always read to you,' her mother asserted. 'I went to a lot of trouble getting Urdu picture books.'

'There's lots of them now,' said Amina. 'Some have dual texts, Urdu one side, English the other.'

'You get nowhere if you can't read,' said Mr Khan. 'You know, I left school in Pakistan when I was ten. But I could read by then. And I read and I read. I simply taught myself. Reading is prime.' He waved his finger vigorously. 'And I'm all for women's education. Ignorant women give you ignorant children.'

'I do so agree,' said Aklis. 'We've encouraged both our daughters in their education.'

'Inaya works in Forest Gate library,' said Mrs Choudhury proudly. 'And Amina is at the local primary school.'

'I'm only a teaching assistant,' said her daughter. 'I'd like to become a teacher.'

'Might that interfere with having a family?' said Mr Khan.

Amina smiled at him. 'Oh, I'm only twenty-one. Plenty of time for that. But I'm fed up with being bossed around by teachers. And really, they don't know much more than I do.

Everyone says I am really good with children.'

'I've seen her,' said her mother. 'She has so much control. They do exactly what she says.'

'Well, mostly they do. You have to be firm. Insist.' She was suddenly aware she was taking too much of the attention, taking over the conversation. 'But I'm sure you know all that.'

'Yes,' said Mr Khan, 'be firm but don't crush. Do that and you make them so timid and they'll run away from a cat.'

'Some parents are so restrictive,' said Amina. She knew she was gushing a little but this was a hot topic with her. 'Especially with their girls.' She leaned forward as if she was giving secret information. 'They send them to Muslim girls' schools, and all they meet are other Muslim girls and they speak Urdu all day. It's such a narrow upbringing.'

'I'm sure their parents are well meaning,' said Mr Khan. 'They don't want their daughters running wild like western girls. Short skirts, drinking and drugs, out all hours. I've seen them coming out of clubs in Ilford.' He shook his head in disgust. 'Shocking.'

Amina was about to speak but her father gave her a reproachful look. So she bit her tongue. You have to be careful with guests. She suspected a business dealing of some sort was going on.

'Progress but modesty with it,' said Mrs Choudhury. 'We live in the west now...'

'That doesn't mean we have to take on all their ways,' interjected Mr Khan.

'Or vice versa,' Amina couldn't stop herself saying.

Mr Khan nodded. 'I agree. Balance is the key. Not so easy. Children tug and pull, want to do this and that before they are ready, as if we know nothing at all.'

'That's what's been lost in this country by the English,' said Aklis, 'parental respect.'

Amina would have liked to have left them at it; go to her

room. But that would be rude. They'd be talking about Pakistan in a minute. What was so good there, and how tough it was for them growing up. She'd heard it all too often. It was a generational thing. She'd been born in this country. Of course, there were bad things about England, but some Muslims it seemed wanted nothing to do with the country at all. At one extreme you had the jihadis and their insane violence. But also the women in burqas. She was told you had to respect the tradition, but there did seem something not quite right in walking down the street, just showing your eyes. That was such a retreat from the clubs of Ilford.

Mr Khan stood up. 'I really must go. It was so nice to have met you all. I shall be in touch.'

Aklis saw him to the door. Amina could hear them still talking in the hallway as Mr Khan put outdoor shoes on.

'What did you think of him?' said her mother.

Amina shrugged. 'Well, fine. A business man. Seems a nice man.'

'He's a multi millionaire,' said her mother. 'With the biggest emporium on Green Street, you know the one, near Plashet Grove. Also a big store in Dalston and another in Birmingham. And what else, I don't know, but he is rich beyond riches.'

'Fancy that,' said Amina. 'Why did he come here?'

'Can't you guess?'

Amina had a horrible thought, but surely it couldn't be that.

'I can't imagine,' she said flatly. 'Tell me.'

Her mother beamed. 'To see if you might make a suitable wife. Think of that.' Her mother clapped her hands. 'A multi millionaire in the family! You would want for nothing.'

'I don't understand,' said Amina, her head wild, trying to grasp the implications. 'I've talked with you and Dad a little about marriage, but nothing specific. Just thoughts. And suddenly you spring this on me.'

Her mother sighed. 'Things have not been going well with your father. In fact, very badly. So badly, we would lose the house if we don't get money...'

'Lose the house?' exclaimed Amina. 'How can that be?'

'It's come to that. Believe me. Bad deals your father has made. The business climate, loans being foreclosed. Your father has been in such a state, but now it all depends...' She indicated the hallway where conversation was still going on.

Amina felt pummelled, in such turmoil she could barely speak. This tea party had been an introduction. She had come in off the street, her mother dressed to the nines, suspecting nothing, and walked into tea and cakes and polite conversation. And it was all a cover for marriage negotiations.

Her father came in skipping, obviously over the moon, rubbing his hands.

'He says yes, it's on. You are a charming young lady and he is willing to marry you.'

'Wonderful!' said Mrs Choudhury.

Amina looked at her parents in their ecstasy, incredulous. She could not believe this was happening. So arranged, so quick.

'He's old,' she muttered.

'Not old at all,' insisted her father. 'Only 53.'

'That's older than you,' she snapped back. 'He's fat, he's bald...' She shook a finger furiously, 'and I know, I know, I know. He's a multi millionaire.' She paused for an instant then threw up her hands, 'Why isn't he married already?'

'He's a widower,' said her father. 'His wife died three years ago. He has grown up children...'

'Older than me, I bet you!' She glared at them both. 'What bear pit are you throwing me into?'

Her mother said carefully, 'We have considered all this,

Amina. But he is not elderly, he is a kind man. In good health. And your family is in trouble.'

'There is no other way out,' said her father. 'This house would have to go otherwise. And maybe everything else. I might just hang on to the Green Street shop but even that wouldn't be certain. This morning, I went with your mother to talk to the imam, I was at my wits' end...' He threw his hands up in triumph. 'And then a couple of phone calls. And I can hardly believe it. Wasif Khan comes over. So much, so quick.'

'Marriage is not part of my plan. Not for another five years or more,' said Amina. 'I want to be a teacher.'

'We all have dreams,' said her mother, 'but real life changes things. You will be a rich man's wife.'

'You're not listening to me,' exclaimed her daughter. 'I want my own life, do you hear me? I don't want to marry a fat, elderly man, more than 30 years my senior, with children older than me who will taunt me the instant he brings me into his house. Oh, I know about these things! I'm not going to be picked off a shelf like a pot. Some pretty young thing to warm his bed in his old age. This is not Pakistan. I have my own life to lead.'

'And just who do you think you are!' yelled her father. 'Me, me, me – that is all you can think of.'

He was charging about the room, throwing his arms about, exclaiming to the walls and ceiling.

'Your selfish desires, my girl, you think they are all that matter? You are part of a family, Amina. Your mother and I brought you up to show respect – and now you throw it all back at us, like some selfish brat living on the pavement.' He thrust his face into hers and shook her shoulders. 'We have given you a good life. You've had whatever you wanted. Do you want to see your parents living on the streets? You ungrateful guttersnipe!'

'This is nothing but forced marriage,' said Amina, wildly

looking about for escape. 'It's illegal in this country.'

Her mother slapped her face. 'Don't you dare talk like that to your parents!'

Amina rocked with the smart of it, her eyes welled. But she would not break down or they would win. She rose and pushed her mother back into the sofa.

'I am not a slave girl,' she shrieked. 'I will not be bartered to save your face. How dare you do this to me!'

And she ran from them. Out of the room, slamming the door hard behind her. She grabbed her outdoor shoes but didn't stop to put them on. And was out the front door, running down the path, on to the pavement, where she could weep, her face stinging, the world tumbling about her head.

Chapter 20

Jack was almost finished on the roof when Amina came past on the street below. He was astride the ridge, moving the roof ladder to the skylight for the last time. He called to her but she didn't seem to hear. He saw her stop to change her shoes, and thought that odd. In fact, her whole behaviour was odd. She went one way, then half a minute later came back and went to Jan's. Well, why not? Neighbours. But so indecisive. It was when he saw her parents come out of the house dressed as if they were going to a wedding, look up and down the street and spot their daughter going into Jan's, that he had an inkling of what was going on. A family row, surely. Mr Choudhury was all for going after her, but his wife held him back. He could hear the husband and wife arguing but it was all in Urdu. Jack didn't call to them; certain it wouldn't be welcomed. The Choudhurys went back inside.

So what had Amina done that had made her parents so angry? He surmised boyfriend trouble. It was usually that sort of thing which made parents blow their tops. Some unsuitable boy. Except it didn't seem right for Amina, her life so enclosed. But then with the internet, who knew who she could be speaking to in her bedroom. A boy from a different religion maybe. Oh! that could put a match to the powder keg.

And she'd gone to Jan's. Not to a relative or a friend. Well, you might say Jan was a friend but a very recent one. But surely, the factor was that Jan wasn't a Muslim. Or was he being too clever? No doubt Jan was getting chapter and verse. All the shabby little details. He was going over for dinner later, so he'd find out soon enough.

Families!

His own mum and dad had separated, so he could talk. Mum had gone all religious, Dad had remarried. He'd got in touch with her but not with him. All because of his drunken days, making enemies of everyone. It embarrassed him to think of all the insults given, the rows he'd had, most of which he knew nothing about until told afterwards. Once in recovery, he'd set about patching up what he could, but there was still his father. They'd never got on that well which made it harder saying sorry. Perhaps he'd phone him this weekend. If his father still had the same number.

The roof work was done. Packing up time. Could he get the roof ladder in through the skylight? It would be awkward; he'd have to go in the skylight first and somehow manoeuvre the ladder so he could draw it into the loft. Even if he could get it in, then he'd have to get it out of the loft. All hassle, and it might end up half in and half out. Best leave it on the roof. Sort it out tomorrow with Jan. Have her at the foot of the double extension ladder, then he could safely go up and bring the roof ladder down without any risk.

His phone rang. His daughter.

'Hello, Mia. I'm in trouble with your mum again.'

'She came to pick me up at school. She was so angry.'

'I suppose it's humiliating for a head teacher.'

'I had to go to her school with her, and sit in her office until the end of the school day. It was dead boring. More boring even than lessons.'

'Where are you now?'

'At your place.'

'That'll make her even madder.'

He was suddenly aware of himself, on the ridge of a roof making a phone call. A woman coming past was looking up at him peculiarly.

'I think she's at peak madness already,' said Mia.

'She's banned me from seeing you.'

'But she hasn't banned me from seeing you.'

Jack scratched his head at this conundrum.

'You haven't got much food in the house,' she went on.

'I wasn't expecting you. Besides, I'm going out for dinner.'

'Another girlfriend?'

He hesitated then said, 'Yes.'

'They never last.'

She sounded just like Alison. Not that it wasn't true, but he would rather not be reminded.

'I'll be back in half an hour,' he said.

But Jack was longer than planned getting home. It wasn't simply a matter of collecting tools. He realised that he couldn't leave the broken skylight open to the elements. If there was a storm in the night then rainwater coming into the loft could soak through to the ceilings below. So he did a temporary bodge, using a couple of thick plastic bags and lots of masking tape, to cover the skylight. Tomorrow he'd get some glass and do a proper repair job.

As extra insurance, he laid out a large plastic sheet on the floor of the loft, reckoning that if the bags over the skylight leaked then the sheet would retain the water. But if there was a big downpour, the rainwater might simply flow off the sheet. So he spent further time building up the sides of the sheet, so it was more like a paddling pool, using pegs and paint cans and whatever he could find in the garden and the back of his van.

So stupid, so unnecessary. He'd need to buy some glass tomorrow for the window.

Jack was about to leave when the lorry turned up with the paving stones, sand and mortar. He and the driver carried the paving stones and the various bags into the drive of 72. There was a car there, so they put the materials well to the side. Jack wondered which of the anarchists owned the car. Black, newer than his van. And so what? It was nothing to him what they'd liberated.

He drove home at last. He wasn't worried about Mia; she'd probably be watching TV, though he did need to shop but couldn't now, delayed as he was. There'd be Alison to deal with of course; the last thing she'd said to him was that Mia wasn't staying with him anymore. Not that he wanted his daughter staying tonight, with dinner arranged at Jan's, but not a blanket ban.

He'd have a chat with Mia, find out exactly what happened at school, then phone Alison and get her to come over. And apologise like mad. Or he could drive Mia there, depending whether Alison was at home or still at school.

Parking was tricky on his road in the evenings. Everyone seemed to park here, plus all the big houses with their multiple tenancies made it like a game of musical chairs. Except the music never stopped and there were no prizes. Just a parking spot, if you were lucky.

He found a space about 100 metres away and walked up to his house, working out what he'd say to Alison. A simple plan, that had to be reconsidered as soon he turned his key in the lock of his flat. There were two voices inside.

'Hello, Jack,' said Alison, as he entered the sitting room.

Mia was on the sofa, her school bag next to her. The TV was on mute. Alison was seated at the table, a teapot and three mugs laid out.

'That saves me a phone call,' he said.

'Tea?' said Alison. He nodded and Alison poured out into the already milked cups. 'That's the last of your milk.'

'Fine,' he said. The least of his problems. He was aware the room was somewhat untidy. And Alison must have seen all the crockery piled in the sink when she went in the kitchen. 'I would have tidied up if I'd known I was going to get visitors.'

'Half eleven last night,' said Alison as she handed round the mugs.

'It was educational,' said Mia. 'There was a Newtonian, a Massukov Cassegrain, and a refractor...'

'Speak English,' said her mother.

Mia sighed deeply at her mother's ignorance. 'Three telescopes. That one.' She indicated the corner where Jack's scope huddled. 'And two others, including a brilliant refractor belonging to Mr Choudhury. I've never seen Archimedes so sharp.'

Jack was amused to see his ex so befuddled. It was everyday stuff if you were keen on astronomy, Greek if you weren't.

'I took a picture on my phone,' went on Mia. 'Do you want to see it?'

'Show me.'

Mia fiddled with her phone, then passed it to her mother.

'The crater in the middle is Archimedes, that range of mountains is called the Apennines.'

Jack stood over them. The picture was good for a camera just held to the eyepiece of the telescope.

'I've also got one of Saturn and its rings,' said Mia. 'It's quite titchy but you can see them.' She flicked to the photo. 'There. You can just see the rings.'

'It's good,' said Alison reluctantly. 'And what's that dot, there?'

'I think it's Titan,' said Mia. 'The largest moon of Saturn. Though it could be a smudge. This is only a phone picture.'

'Show me the moon one again.'

Mia flicked back to it. Jack could see Alison struggling with degrees of sinfulness. Education – ten out of ten. Late night – zero.

'I am pleased my daughter is so keen on astronomy,' she said at last. 'I'm a teacher, I see plenty of dumb kids who play computer games all night... But half eleven? That's really not on, Jack. I had to go in and get her. Me, a head teacher! Though frankly, if they'd let her sleep for half an hour I'm sure she would have been fine.'

Mia winked at Jack. He didn't wink back as Alison would have seen, but it was clear he was off the hook.

'It won't happen again,' he said. 'Any future telescope sessions will only be at weekends or school holidays.'

'OK,' said Alison. 'And can you please wash your dishes from time to time?'

Chapter 21

Inaya left the house. It had been quite a conversation she'd just had with her parents. Well, hardly a conversation, she had simply listened. To her father's dodgy dealing, without the actual details, and then blaming the recession and ruthless competitors for his downfall. And then swiftly, like a conjuror's legerdemain pulling out a dove, to the way out favoured by both parents, but not by Amina.

Inaya had seen Wasif Khan from afar. It had been at an Asian fashion show at his Green Street shop. He, seated in the front row, had been pointed out to her as the owner. She was well back in the many rows of seats. She hadn't actually seen much more than the back of his head but in her mind's eye brought in the body and the face, as her parents told of his qualities, emphasising the financial. These were considerable, heightened in the light of the current Choudhury problems.

But to marry him? That was a leap. Inaya was grateful she was about to be married as surely, if she were free, she would be first in line. And what would you have done in that case, her mother had asked her. Marry him, she'd replied at once.

She'd been sent to talk sense into Amina. As her older sister and nearer her age, her parents had said, you might get through to her. Amina had gone to that illustrator woman, Jan. Inaya had met her at the telescope party; she seemed nice enough, but that was just one evening and everyone had been on best behaviour. Now Jan had her sister. That kafir woman, her father had said. Not a nice thing to say. Unclean, an unbeliever. The lines were drawn. Not that she went in for that stuff. Working in the library, you just couldn't. She had to treat all believers equally and even unbelievers. Of course, once you were home, behind closed doors, words might be said, but more often for members of their own community, than outsiders. Jan was simply English as far as she was concerned, and couldn't be condemned for that.

She rang the bell, adjusting her hijab as she did not know if any men were in the house. Jan was friends with that builder, she knew. In fact, Inaya suspected that Jan might be his girlfriend. Nothing to do with her. The English had different ways. She was nervous, not knowing how she'd be received. It was not a usual thing for her to ring the doorbells of people she barely knew, and English at that.

Jan opened the door. She was wearing a white T-shirt and jeans, and was bare-footed.

'Hello, Inaya,' said Jan.

'I wondered if I might talk to my sister.'

Jan leaned forward and said quietly, 'She's very upset.'

'That's what I want to talk to her about. If you don't mind.'

Jan thought for a moment, then said, 'I'll ask her if it's alright. One moment. Won't be a minute.'

She left the door open a little, and went inside. Inaya could of course have barged in. Her father would have done. Well, in the state he was now, no doubt about that. Perhaps her mother? Or certainly insisted her way in. But Inaya would accept a yes or a no. And if it was no, hand the situation back to her parents.

Jan returned. 'Amina will talk to you. Please come in.'

Inaya entered. She slipped off her shoes automatically and noted that Amina's were against the wall by the door. Jan led her into the kitchen where her sister was sitting on a high stool drinking coffee.

'I'll leave you two to talk,' said Jan. 'I'll be in my work room, if you need me.'

And she left them.

'Nice place she's got,' said Inaya, looking around the kitchen with its dark wood and glass units, grained marble worktops and the usual white kitchen goods. There was a colourful abstract painting on one wall, on the other a large cork board covered in bits of paper stuck on with drawing pins.

'So they've told you everything?' queried Amina.

Inaya nodded and sat on a stool. 'Everything. It was a total shock.'

Amina gave a half smile. 'Daddy's financial dealings or my reaction?'

'The fact that we'd lose the house,' said Inaya. 'That things had got so bad. We've lived there all our lives. It's home.'

'Not for you much longer.'

'It's still home.'

'Coffee?' said Amina. It was as if she were the host, having been here an hour longer.

'Yes, please.'

There was a half-filled cafetiere and a milk jug on the table between them. Amina took a cup off a hook and poured coffee.

'So they sent you to persuade me,' said Amina, handing over the coffee. 'Help yourself to milk.'

'They thought Jan wouldn't let them in,' she said. 'And thought I might have a better effect.'

'Have you seen Wasif Khan?'

'Not close up. Last year I saw him at a fashion show, but I didn't pay much attention.'

'He's fat, bald and 53.'

'That's not so old.'

'Seven years older than Dad. 32 years older than me.'

The maths were unarguable.

'He's got millions upon millions,' said Inaya.

'I know. That's his prime asset.' She paused for a second then added, 'Would you marry him?'

'That's what Mum asked me.'

'And what did you say?'

'I said I would.'

Amina blew a raspberry. 'Easy to say that when you are marrying Ahmed in two weeks.'

'To tell you the truth,' said Inaya, 'I am so glad this happened now and not three months ago. Not glad for you, but being utterly selfish... My marriage is now going to happen. It's like a train, all the arrangements made, hundreds of guests invited, too much has been spent, it's unstoppable. Besides, no one outside of the family circle will know about our crisis until the wedding is well over. But if this had happened say December, it would have killed my marriage, I'm sure.'

'It's all property and money, isn't it? Like *Pride and Prejudice.*'

'Not quite. I love Ahmed.'

'Lucky that. But his family sized us up and we sized them up. I remember Dad making enquiries.'

'I'm grateful he did. I don't want to end up on the top floor of a council tower block.'

They were silent a while, drinking their coffees.

'Do you think I should marry Wasif Khan?' said Amina.

Inaya looked directly at her sister. 'Yes,' she said. 'For the good of the family.'

Amina threw up her hands. 'Oh, you disgust me, Inaya. You are so cowardly. It's safe to side with Mum and Dad. Don't rock the boat. In fact, smoother for you and your own marriage.'

'You'd want for nothing for the rest of your life...'

'Except an attractive husband, my own age, except someone I have some feeling for... Do you know he has grown-up children? How will they treat me?'

'I'm sure that could be sorted out,' said Inaya uncomfortably. 'It won't be that bad. Think of a big house with servants.'

'And what will I do all day? Wait for hubby to come home while I boss the cook and gardener? I want to be a teacher...'

'And you think you can be if you leave home like this?'

They were silent. How could her sister be a teacher? She'd need money, somewhere to live, while she was training. And be utterly cut off from her family. The last thing Inaya wanted was for the family home to be sold. She'd have to deal with the recriminations, accusations of bad faith from her in-laws.

'Marry him. For the good of the family, Amina.'

Amina put up her hands. 'Enough. Leave me alone. Tell Mum and Dad I'm not going to marry him. No ifs, no buts, make it absolutely clear.' She stopped, was obviously considering something. 'I need some clothes. Who's at home right now?'

'Just Mum.'

'I'll go back with you and pick some things up.'

Chapter 22

Alison took Mia away. They'd arranged Mia would come over to Jack's on Saturday morning. After they had left, he washed up, knowing he'd got off lightly. But then Alison needed Jack as much as he needed her. Divorced they may be, but they had a daughter to bring up. Not so good for her to be carted back and forth, but better than being dumped on strangers.

Alison had told him that she'd made an offer on the Sebert Road house, less than a mile from where he lived. What complications might that involve if she got it? So easy to drop in, for mother or daughter. To get involved again in each other's lives. On balance, he preferred Alison at a distance, but even if the offer was accepted, the machinations of the lawyers would take several months. Forget it, till it was a fact.

He considered vacuuming the sitting room, and hesitated for half a minute before he moved a few papers onto a pile in the corner. And went to have a shower. By the time he came out, the thought had been washed away in soapy water and he did an hour's accounts before heading off for Jan's.

Jack decided to take the van as he knew he'd be staying the night. It hadn't been stated as such but it was assumed by both parties. There was no point wasting time walking back for the van in the morning.

It was still light when he left, though the lights were on in the high street as he drove over, reminding him to turn on his headlights. It was a load off his mind to sort out Mia with Alison. He hated rows and would do a lot to avoid them. Generally his ex was sensible. Except when it came to her love life, and then she was unpredictable. Almost as bad as he was himself. She was tough though. You couldn't be a pushover if you wanted to be a head teacher. Just a pity she had a habit of slamming into him.

Jack, on arrival, found Jan pensive. She led him into the kitchen where she was cooking, making him think he should have brought some chocolates or flowers. He might have done if he hadn't been so hassled today. Too bad. She didn't seem to mind, though you never knew. She was stirring the frying pan, wearing a floral apron. There was a smell of fried onions and peppers, his stomach curled at the odours, reminding him that he must do some shopping.

She said, as she tipped in garlic from the crusher, 'I'm worried about Amina. She left with her sister to pick up some clothes over an hour ago. She said she'd just be ten minutes.'

'What was all that about?' he said.

Jan hesitated, undecided whether to continue cooking or to seriously talk, then turned off the gas and took off her apron. She settled on a high stool opposite him and joined him in a coffee while filling him in on what she knew about the Choudhurys' affairs.

'I knew something was up,' he said when she'd done. 'From up on the roof, I saw Amina come running out of the house and come here, saw her parents looking for her... Quite a tale.'

'I told her she could stay here a while.' Jan shrugged, waving a vague hand. 'However long a while is. A week, I don't know. And then her sister came to speak to her. I left them to it. And the pair left together, Amina telling me she'd be back in ten minutes or so. That was...' She looked at the kitchen clock. 'Over 75 minutes ago.'

'Have you tried phoning?'

'Just before you came. Her phone's off.'

'We don't know what deal they've come to,' said Jack. 'Maybe her parents have backed down.'

'I'm just worried,' said Jan. 'You'd think, having involved me, she'd tell me what she was up to, wouldn't you?'

But they agreed there was nothing they could do. Amina was an adult and could make her own decisions. And if she was forgetful, perhaps she had cause.

Jan recommenced cooking. A vegetabley, meaty fry up, the pasta bubbling away. Jack was salivating as he watched her stirring the pan. He'd not eaten since lunchtime, and had been busy ever since, what with work, Alison and Mia, even the washing up. Besides which, he had nothing at home to eat. He wondered if he dared ask for a slice of bread to tide him over? Decided best not to. Alison was touchy about such things. Jan might be too. He could hold out for another twenty minutes.

Chapter 23

They were drinking coffee after dinner when there was a ring on the bell.

'Amina – do you think?' said Jan as she rose to go to the door.

Through the glass of the front door, she could see it wasn't her. Too tall, no hijab. She sighed; she really didn't want visitors. An evening with Jack, that had been her plan. She cautiously opened up.

It was Tosh with a scruffy pile of papers, scratching his stubby hair with his free hand as if he had fleas.

'I don't know whether this is convenient,' he said, 'but I brought my comic...'

She was about to send him away, but could see he was trembling. Experience said his comic would be poor roughs. She'd been here before, too often, looking at pictures at book fairs when some keen fan brought them along for her expert opinion, and she trying hard not to offend.

'I can give you ten minutes,' she said at last. 'No longer.'

'That'll do,' he said. 'I know you've got an eye, having seen your work.'

'You don't need to flatter me,' she said wrinkling her nose. 'Just come in.'

She led him through to the kitchen. Seeing Jack, Tosh said: 'I can see I've interrupted your evening. I don't want to be a nuisance, I can come back some other time.'

'What you here for, Tosh?' said Jack, in no hurry to move, having fully stoked up.

'Just my comic,' he said, indicating the papers he was carrying. 'Jan promised to look at it, and I thought I'd bring it over.'

'Let's clear some space on the table,' said Jan. And she began moving plates and serving dishes to the side of the sink and on to the units, Jack helping by passing items over.

Tosh was standing awkwardly, shuffling from foot to foot.

'Take a stool,' said Jack. 'There's still some coffee...'

'If you don't mind,' said Tosh, sitting down.

Jack poured him a coffee and passed him the milk jug. Jan wiped the table, thinking what to say to someone who has worked hard, but whose work simply isn't up to professional standard. She could suggest he did an illustrating course. Or simply say the work showed promise. It was never easy saying face to face what you really thought, but there was nothing to be gained for her in tearing strips off the young man. It wasn't as if she were buying.

Tosh spread out his pictures on the table. They were all in black, no colour at all. She was struck immediately by the clarity and energy. They were political, a history of anarchy in pictures.

'These are good,' said Jack.

'Thanks,' said Tosh but he was really waiting for Jan, watching her intently, his hands shaking.

'It's really organised,' said Jack. 'Like a real comic. I wish I could draw like that.'

Jan scanned them, taking in the table that was now covered in the comic, then went to the first page.

'This is good stuff,' she said truthfully, almost with relief. So much easier to praise real skill, than search to find something encouraging about substandard work. 'I was expecting rubbish and working out how to say something nice... But I don't have to. This is fantastic.'

'You mean it?'

'I do. I don't agree with your politics. But the pictures are good enough to keep me reading in spite of that.'

Tosh was beaming.

'You get so much movement in these images. And the

faces are dynamic. You've got variety. And you switch the angles beautifully. Why just black ink?'

Tosh shrugged. 'Cheaper, but also I thought different. Everything's colour these days. Also gives that old fashioned feel. Colour means capitalism.'

Jan smiled. She used lots of colour and she made money too.

'I love them,' she said. 'And I have some ideas, but I don't want to say anything until I've had a proper look. Can you leave them with me, and I'll go through them tomorrow?'

'Happy to,' said Tosh.

'How about coming over at five tomorrow, and we'll discuss them properly. I can then give them my full attention. That's what they deserve.'

'Sure. I'm really glad you like my work.'

'You've got talent,' she said. 'You're an illustrator. And I am so pleased to have met you. I tell you, on my travels I have met lots of scrawlers who haven't a clue...'

Tosh had risen. 'Only Susie has seen it. She likes my stuff, but you can't trust your girlfriend, can you? Not for an honest opinion. I mean she just wants to please you... That's why what you've said means so much.'

'It's good, really good.' Jan couldn't take her eyes off the work. This was so different from her own work. She had her niche. She was known, but she couldn't draw like this. The detail, the sweep, the free energy of line.

She looked up at last and piled the papers together. 'Tomorrow,' she said. 'I really look forward to giving it some time.' Then a thought. 'We've lots of food left over. Do you want to take it next door?'

'Whatever you've got,' said Tosh eagerly. 'All we've got is bread and peanut butter.'

Jan gathered the bits and pieces from her cooking pots and scooped them into plastic boxes.

'How long have you been working on this?' said Jack,

indicating the pile of papers.

'About six months on and off,' said Tosh. 'Good ink is so expensive.'

'I've got plenty,' said Jan, 'but we'll sort that out tomorrow.' She handed over three plastic boxes with their lids on. 'Get these over straight away, while the food is warm.'

'You couldn't lend us three plates?' he said wistfully.

'What do you eat off?' she exclaimed, getting three plates down from the cupboard, and as an afterthought added forks. She could see he was getting overloaded, so put them in a carrier bag and handed it to him.

'Thanks for your time and the food,' he said as he took her offering. 'Have a good evening, Jack.'

'You too, mate.'

She accompanied Tosh along the hallway. At the door she said to him, 'What do you know about what Anton did to me today?'

Tosh hesitated on the front step, then said, 'He told us he was just having a game.'

'He could've killed me.'

'I'm sure he never meant that.'

She would have said more but felt that Tosh would simply defend his colleague. She'd ask again tomorrow, not while he was leaving.

'See you tomorrow afternoon,' she said with a half smile. 'And bring the boxes back.' As an afterthought as he was walking up the path, she called, 'You can keep the plates and forks a while.'

She returned to the kitchen.

'That was a surprise,' said Jack.

'I'm quite jealous,' she said. 'His work is so dynamic. It makes my Space Cat feel even more tired.'

'So what are you going to do?'

'Introduce him to my publisher.'

Chapter 24

Tosh served the food out, on to the three plates given to him by Jan. He was careful to be as equal as possible in the portions. He let Anton and Susie take theirs first, and took the one remaining.

'So what'd the bitch have to say?' said Anton with a forkful of pasta, the plate in his lap.

'Do you have to call every woman a bitch?' exclaimed Susie.

'She is not every woman,' said Anton, spearing a piece of meat. 'She is a woman in a big house, making a pile out of her kids' books.'

'You're happy to eat her food,' said Susie. 'Off her plates.'

'I am not going to touch my forelock for a bit of pasta and meat,' said Anton. 'She's a capitalist bitch.'

'Jan is alright,' said Tosh.

'Because she said a few nice things about your pictures?'

'She was genuinely nice, Anton. Allow that. She talked to me about my efforts and she didn't have to. She gave us this food without me asking for it. Jesus.'

'The bourgeoisie can be very seductive,' said Anton, conceding nothing, as he stoked his grub in as if someone was about to pull it away. 'Beware, Tosh. Historically the ruling class have given the proletariat treats since the year dot. A harvest supper, a Christmas party for the children, a charabanc to the seaside... All to blind the gullible schmucks to their daylight robbery.'

'Why did you try to kill her?' said Tosh.

'I didn't. Just give her a scare.'

'She says it was more than that.'

'She would, wouldn't she?'

Tosh was infuriated with Anton. He was such a hard liner, so unforgiving. Or maybe Anton was right, and he was easily seduced. A few kind words, though he did feel she was being honest with him. He needed to work this out. Was it the individual or was it the system? Anton would say both, but Tosh wasn't so sure. We are all part of the system whether we want to be or not. Either way, he liked Jan. And he was seeing her tomorrow afternoon.

They ate in silence a while. The food was good, even if prepared by an arch-capitalist, the meat and vegetables well-seasoned, and such a change to have some salad. Too long on their diet and Tosh was sure they'd die of scurvy like 18th century sailors in the South Seas.

'So you know what to do tomorrow, Susie?' said Anton, putting down his empty plate and wiping his mouth with his sleeve.

'Wait for my men to return like a good housewife,' she said peevishly.

They'd had this one out earlier. Anton and Tosh were doing the raid. She'd argued why did it have to be the two men. The fact that Tosh could drive, and she couldn't, was the decider.

'So what do you do when we get back to the house?' he said.

'I change the number plates on the car,' she said with a weary sigh. 'Pronto. Then I help you two bandits wash the paint off your faces. Every bit, off ears, nose and neck.'

'Is it racist?' mused Tosh, 'to brown up?'

'We're not a minstrel show singing to whitey for our supper,' exclaimed Anton, throwing up his hands in mock despair. 'We're doing a bank robbery for the revolution.'

'But we're reflecting the black stereotype.'

'Stop playing professor,' spat Anton. 'There's CCTV at the bank. They will see two Asian men. And as soon as we get back here, wigs off, soap and water, and we'll be part of the Caucasian majority.'

'I'm not sure about my wig,' muttered Tosh.

Anton laughed. 'We can't have you browned up with your blond hair, now can we? Or is it you want to look good on TV?'

Susie collected the plates and put the three plastic boxes together.

'I'll wash them,' said Tosh.

'You brought the food over and served it out,' she said. 'Anton should wash up for once.'

'I got the car,' he said, poking himself on the chest. 'I've done all the organising for tomorrow including gun, car, wigs and grease paint...'

'Is washing up for servants then?'

He stared at her as if about to quote some holy scripture, then said, 'Never let it be said I don't do my share of the chores.' He picked up the boxes and plates and headed out. 'After the revolution, we are all servants, we are all bosses.'

He left them.

'Anton does make me want to scream,' she exclaimed, once sure he was out of earshot. 'Everything is about the revolution. The woman next door is a capitalist bitch, the washing up is only to be done if it furthers revolutionary aims... I'll be so glad when the others move in.'

'Just a couple of days, sweetheart,' said Tosh. 'Once the raid's done with, we can be a real collective. I mean just the three of us...' He guffawed. 'It's no better than the nuclear family.'

Chapter 25

Jack had breakfast at Jan's. She had a full larder, unlike his own Mother Hubbard effort. He must do some shopping today. He couldn't even offer Alison a biscuit yesterday. Still, as she didn't expect him to have any, she wasn't disappointed. Though it would have been nice to surprise her. And he should pay the anarchists £125, half their £250, as Terry had paid him half the bill.

But he begrudged them the cash. Anton had pushed for it, but Anton was a rat. He'd pulled the ladder away from Jan; it had to be him. And for what reason? The fact that she was well-off, a property owner, and up there on 'his' roof which was almost funny, if it wasn't murderous. But it did mean Jack would have to take every precaution when retrieving his roof ladder. He was sure Anton could come up with a reason for murdering him, anything to further the revolution. Though if he were to survive the great rising of the people, he'd be lined up against the wall with the rest of the self-employed, with Anton manning the machine gun.

Half of him saw Anton as a joke, the other half wanted to throw him off a cliff. He mustn't get so wound up but concentrate on the work in hand. Before anything else he had to buy glass and putty. He should deduct this from the anarchists' two fifty. In fact, he worked out as he drove, he should deduct fifty quid, covering materials and labour for the window. That got them down to two hundred. And to hell with it, he wouldn't give them any unless he had to. Unearned income, they were against that, weren't they?

Should he return the money to Terry, if he avoided paying the anarchists? Well, as Terry didn't know it was an overcharge, then Terry wouldn't miss it. Besides, it was the smallest of small change to someone who could leave a big house empty, and was taking no steps whatsoever to evict the squatters. Jack failed to understand the very rich. They seemed never to have enough, but could leave a house empty. It was beyond him. Was it a tax fiddle?

There were several builders in front of him at the glazier's. Everyone wanted their glass first thing. Maybe he should've gone later in the day. He could've got on with the patio and come here at lunchtime. Except he was here now, and would get served in the end. He looked at his watch. All the time swallowed up in buying materials.

Jan had said she'd keep a lookout for Amina when she left for school. He wondered what had happened. Most likely her parents had backed down. He felt sorry for them, but it wasn't fair to load all Aklis's bad deals on Amina.

With the glass he set off for 72.

Susie let him in with a grunt. Maybe she'd slept badly. He shrugged it off, at least he was in. He went upstairs with the glass and his toolbox. His stepladder was in the top hallway. Everything he needed to get this loss maker out of the way. More than an hour of the working day had gone already.

And another hour went by in putting the glass in. He worked from the loft, first chipping the remnants of glass out and scraping off the old putty. All set for the new. It was an annoying, unnecessary job, but the sooner done with, the sooner he could earn money.

The glass in, he went next door to pick up Jan. They had a coffee, and she made him a bacon sandwich. He felt he deserved it, having been working more than two hours already. Jan had been sketching. She was wearing old jeans this morning and an old sweat shirt. She'd remembered to put on her boots, and had kept the hard hat overnight.

They climbed over Jan's fence and onto the patio of 72. Jack put up the double extension ladder, checking the stand-off was firm and the sandbag held the bottom. Jan had a small camera with her. She insisted that he take a photograph of her. She stood, one foot on the bottom rung of the ladder, holding a rung over her head while he took a couple of pictures. She did look attractive, her jeans more figure hugging than his loose attire, the yellow helmet suiting her complexion, her hair to her shoulders.

She insisted that she needed a few more photos for her Facebook page. Jack sighed at this and wheelbarrowed in some paving stones for props. She picked one up, straining to hold it.

'Quick, get the picture, before I collapse.'

Then a few more of Jan pushing the wheelbarrow.

'Now how about we do some work?' he said, barely hiding his impatience. He handed her the camera. She blew a raspberry at him, then smiled.

Jack looked at his watch. 'I haven't earned a penny yet today,' he exclaimed, 'and it's getting on for eleven.'

'Oh, you slave driver!'

'Just keep an eye on the ladder,' he said, 'and no sarky comments.'

'I don't think Anton is in anyway,' she said. 'I've only seen Susie about.'

'Watch to be on the safe side.' And he began to climb.

At the top, he looked over his roof work. The new tiles blended in well, there were no loose ones. So he hadn't missed any. The new glass in the skylight gleamed in the morning sun. Job done up here. He raised the hook of the roof ladder over the roof ridge, turned it over until it rested on its wheels, and then drew it down the roof, until he could hold it in one hand. And then climbed back down to ground level.

At the bottom, as he turned, still holding the roof ladder, Jan snapped a picture.

'For your new website,' she said.

He put down the roof ladder, and they took down the

extension ladder. They carried them off the patio and laid them on the lawn out of the way.

'That's the roof work done,' he said.

'Thank goodness for that,' said Jan.

'Let's get started on the patio.'

They came in and out of the house, along the hallway, about half a dozen times, ferrying paving stones and the bags of mortar and sand. Jan insisted on taking more photos. For the website, she said. They put the materials at the end of the patio between 72 and the Choudhury house.

'The aim is to do both patios today,' he said. 'Photo-shoot permitting.'

'Cool it, Jack,' she exclaimed. 'I said I'd redo your website. OK? Well, I need photos for it.'

He conceded he was being unjust. It was all the time wasted on the window that really irked him.

'Point taken.'

The fence between the two houses was wooden with concrete posts between the sections. The fencing slotted into recesses in the posts. Jack and Jan together lifted out one section of fencing, so they could get in and out of both gardens easily.

When they'd laid the fencing section on the lawn of 74, Jan saw Amina. She tapped Jack on the shoulder.

'That's why she didn't come back last night.'

Jack turned and looked up to the first floor window. Amina was there, having opened the lacy nets, without her hijab, her hair to her shoulders. In front of her, she held a piece of paper to the window glass. It said: I AM A PRISONER.

PART FOUR: PRISONERS

Chapter 26

Susie kept looking at her watch. It wouldn't make them come any quicker, but she was impatient for this to be over with. Nervous too, it was a risky business. She had everything ready in the print room. All three were to be working on a print job. The new number plates were there for the car, with the tools to do the switch. She had two pristine washing-up bowls full of soapy water, the bowls bought new yesterday with rolls of kitchen towel. The guys were to pull up the car in the parking space, and head straight into the house, remove wigs and wash off the brown greasepaint. She would be outside changing the plates, having set the printer going immediately they came in. She put her fingers in the water of one of the washing-up bowls, it was lukewarm and cooling.

Where were they?

Tosh and Anton were in brown warehouse-coats for the raid, Anton's long hair and Tosh's blond wig covered. Coats and wigs were to be removed as they drove away. And once back here, wash and wash. She'd been worried to see Jack and Jan come so often through the hallway with the wheelbarrow, but now they'd stopped. She'd looked out the back and seen the paving stones and bags of sand. And hoped they'd stay out back, working on the patio.

Should she lock the back door? That would only make them suspicious. Anton had been right about Jan being here. She shouldn't be. And maybe Jack shouldn't be either. The trouble with Anton was that he made such a fuss about everything that it was a big climb down to agree with anything he said.

But then again, Jack had fixed the hot water. And with all

the grease and ink from printing, that was not to be sneezed at. They didn't have to live like sewer rats.

She looked again at her watch. Where were they? The sooner Anton and Tosh got here, brought the money in and got cleaned up, the better for all of them. A slick bank job, that was the plan. In, grab the stuff and away. She'd wanted to be involved, directly, not back here waiting for the boys to come back. It was exciting, going into a bank, challenging everyone with a gun. There, in the blaze of the action, among the moneychangers, the foot-soldiers of capitalism. She'd have liked to have handed out leaflets to the customers in the queue. But, of course, that was impossible. As far as any customers were concerned, they were run of the mill bank robbers, working class capitalists so to speak. She hoped none of them would be stupid enough to interfere. It wasn't their money, after all. They'd lose nothing. So why be foolhardy?

In two days, four more of their group would be joining them here. She could barely wait. It was a big house, far too big for the three of them. But it had been decided there should be only three for the time being, a quiet squat, to attract less attention. Sensible, she supposed, but it would be heaven to dilute Anton's diatribes. And there was a promise of furniture, so they could live like human beings, instead of camping out in a house.

She'd like a washing machine; to hell with Anton and his bourgeois this and bourgeois that. What was so good about having dirty clothes or having to hand-wash them? Her granny had told her about when she was young, doing the washing in the scullery, with a clothes boiler and a washboard. All Monday, nothing but washing she'd said, with hard bars of yellow soap until your hands were red raw. And quite right too, Anton would say. He was a Luddite when it came down to it, not that the Luddites were wrong. Not a Luddite then, maybe a romantic, he'd hate her for saying it, but it was as if manual work in itself were holy. To some extent, she had to admit, they were all somewhat that way, but Anton took it to crazy extremes.

She was at the window, the curtains drawn, peering through a crack. She looked again at her watch. Where were they? They shouldn't be this long, surely? Maybe the money delivery was delayed. Traffic. There were good reasons. How could she know, here?

And then they came, the car speeding and screeching into the drive of the house. She picked up the number plates and tools and rushed out to the front.

By the time she arrived, Anton had opened his side and sped to the other. Something was wrong with Tosh. He was sagging against the door, the wig slipping off his head.

'Help me get him!' yelled Anton.

'What happened?'

Anton had opened the door. Tosh almost fell out. There was blood on the seat.

'A pig's breakfast,' exclaimed Anton. 'This dope got in the way. Get him inside, get him in!'

Chapter 27

They'd put the extension ladder up to Amina's window. Jack climbed, while Jan held the foot. He had a few tools in a cloth bag over his shoulder. Once at the window height, Amina mimed that she couldn't open the window. He'd worked that out anyway. There must be a window-lock with a key, he thought. It would be one hell of a job breaking that, or breaking the frame. It would have to be the glass again.

This time, though, he had a glass cutter. Quieter too, he didn't know who was in the house. Amina had instinctively put her hijab back on. Jack sorted through his tools, laying the glass cutter and a steel ruler on the windowsill. He examined the window, felt along the inside. He would need to cut out the minimum for Amina to get through. She wasn't that big, so maybe a twenty inch square.

The glass cutter had not been used, so had a keen edge. He took it up, felt it with his thumb. Sharp. He etched a line along the bottom, keeping to the wood. Then up the side-wood, twenty inches or so, making two sides of the square, then across the glass along the edge of the steel rule. And lastly, down to meet his original etch. Amina was watching intently, every so often glancing behind her, which told Jack Mum or Dad, or both, were in the house.

He mimed her to press her hands against the piece of glass. She didn't understand at first, so he had to do it himself a couple of times. He didn't want the glass falling to the floor and shattering when it came out. That would alert Mum and Dad. Then she understood, and wisely held a cloth against the glass. Jack gave the glass a sudden push; the square came out and Amina was able to hold it in the cloth, and put it down.

'Oh, am I so pleased to see you,' she murmured.

'Out,' he said. 'We'll talk later.'

He dropped several rungs to give her room to come through. She wasn't in recommended dress for a break out, jeans would be better than salwar kameez. Perhaps she didn't have any. Amina put her legs through first and he helped put her feet on to the rung of the ladder. Then she slowly eased her body through the gap, until her head was out.

Jack came down the ladder, Amina following. Immediately on the ground she rushed to Jan.

'I couldn't even phone you, Jan,' she exclaimed. 'They took it away from me.'

'We'll talk at my place,' said Jan. 'Let's go.'

Jan ushered her through the gap in the fence while Jack was drawing down the ladder. The back door of the house opened, and Aklis came out into the garden in his shirt sleeves.

'What the hell are you up to?' he yelled, looking wildly about him trying to take it all in.

Aklis looked to the window, to the ladder and the fleeing women. They were running across the patio in the next door garden, with Jan tugging Amina along. Aklis ran to the gap in the fence, obviously keen to pursue them, but Jack grabbed him and held him back.

'Let her go!' exclaimed Jack. 'She's an adult.'

'Mind your own damn business, builder!'

He tried to jerk himself away but Jack held his arms. Jan and Amina had gone in the back door of 72. Aklis kicked at Jack who pushed him to the ground. He stared at the prone man for an instant and thought, useless to try reasoning with him. And ran through the fence and into the other garden, after the women.

'Give me back my daughter!' cried Aklis getting to his feet. 'How dare you interfere with my family affairs!'

Jack was running across the patio as Aklis was coming

149

through the fence. He turned at the back door, thought of shutting him out but Aklis was too close. They'd have to get Amina to Jan's place and shut him out. He ran down the hallway of 72, Aklis was coming in. Jack would go straight through and out the front door, catch the women and go into Jan's together. Shut the door on him and let Mr Choudhury ring until doomsday.

Out of the side room came Anton. He had a gun in his hand. Jack stopped in his tracks.

'What's this about?' he said, bewildered.

'This is loaded,' hissed Anton. 'And the safety catch is off. So do as you're told. I will not hesitate to shoot.' He was distracted for an instant with Aklis coming into the hallway. 'Ah, another one. All the better,' he added. 'Let's go in the front room for a chat.'

'Where's my daughter?' yelled Aklis with Jack blocking much of his view of Anton.

Anton fired a shot. Jack leapt back in fear and surprise, bumping into Aklis. Jack managed to keep to his feet and put his hands up. Aklis, who'd been knocked over, scrambled up fearfully, now too aware of his danger, and raised his hands.

'Next time, I won't miss,' said Anton. 'Come and join the family.'

He ushered them both into the long room, standing at the door like a benign host. Once inside, Jack saw Jan and Amina with their hands raised. Susie was crouched down on the ground over a prone Tosh.

'He needs a doctor, Anton,' exclaimed Susie. Her face was smeared, as if she'd been crying.

'One thing at a time.' He waved the gun at his captives. 'Against the wall, you lot. Right against it. Keep those hands high. Come on, against the wall.'

They backed against the wall, facing front, arms high as ordered. Jack could not see the others, not daring to look about him, but could hear their breathing, as fast as his own. What on earth had he walked into?

Anton went to the front window. He peered through the curtains without opening them.

'The cops are here.' He turned to his captives. 'Now we'll have some fun.'

He came back to them from the window, and walked along the line as if inspecting them, the gun held at chest height.

'I've nothing to lose,' he said. 'Get me? I've killed a man already this morning. And I'm quite happy to add one or two more to the list. So do what you're told. I want no talking unless I ask you something. Get me?'

Jack nodded. He believed Anton utterly; he looked like he'd killed. And could kill more. The best thing to do was obey him to the letter. Not thwart him, and hope there'd be a rescue. Anton was walking up and down them, the gun levelled, as if he feared they might make a run for it. He was passing the gun from hand to hand. Not a good situation. Anything could spook him.

'The fuzz could come in shooting,' exclaimed Anton. 'We need to put them in the picture. Let me think.'

'Tosh needs a doctor, Anton,' exclaimed Susie.

'Shut up! How can I think with you bleating?'

'He's unconscious,' she yelled. 'There's blood all over the shop.'

'If you don't shut up, I'll shoot you too, Susie,' he screamed. 'Believe me if I won't!'

The room stilled. The hostages had their backs to the wall, hands fully stretched, not daring to move an inch while Anton did his thinking. He bit his knuckle, scratched his face. His face was brown stained, some attempt at disguise, Jack surmised. Some event that had brought this about, that had brought the cops here. A murder somewhere. Jack pressed against the wall, his arms aching. He could sense the other hostages but did not dare look at them, though he could just see Susie crouched down with Tosh. She was wiping his face, murmuring something or other.

'Someone's got to go out and talk to them,' said Anton as if speaking to himself. He looked along the line of them, considering. 'You, Jack. You've got sense.' He was looking Jack in the eye. Jack looked down, not wanting to appear to challenge him.

'What do you want me to do?' said Jack.

'Tell the cops to stay back, out of sight. Tell them there'll be no shooting then. But if they try to break in, I'll kill the lot of you. Get that?'

'Yes.' It was clear, too clear. Anton was jumpy, and certainly not joking.

'I want you back here in five minutes,' went on Anton, 'or I kill...' His gun traced the line as he looked over his captives. 'Jan. I've never liked you.' He half smiled at her before switching to Jack. 'Five minutes max, Jack. Get me?'

'Yes.'

'And get a doctor please!' exclaimed Susie.

'Yeh, get a doctor,' nodded Anton. He ushered Jack out with the gun. 'On your way. Get those cops to back off. Five minutes. Or Jan is meat. What you waiting for?'

Jack, his hands still held up, headed off. Out of the room, into the hallway and to the front door. He opened the door, the sunlight blinding him for an instant. Then he saw police cars in the road, and men shielding behind them with guns pointing at him.

He put his hands up to show submission, only then realising they would have no idea who he was.

'Don't shoot. I'm just a messenger!' he yelled, hands held as high as he could manage. 'Don't shoot. I'm not with the gunman!'

He slowly walked down the path, watching the men behind the cars in the road, keeping his hands well up. Their guns were all trained on him, following him as he walked towards them. His body was boiling; he wanted to simply run, be away from the loaded guns. But to run was to die. He must walk slowly, no sudden movements, and show them he was no threat.

Out of the gate he came, stepping across the pavement and on into the roadway, where police cars were in the middle of the road. He stepped into a gap between cars, and was immediately dragged behind, further in and thrown to the ground. Several arms were mauling at him, voices yelling.

'On your front! Over, on your front!'

They pushed him over onto his belly, in spite of his yelling, and immediately slapped his wrists into handcuffs. Jack lay still, the handcuffs cutting into his wrists as hands were feeling down his body. They groped in his pockets and took out a tape measure, a glass cutter and several nails. From his shirt pocket a hand drew some of his business cards.

'Stand him up,' called a voice of authority.

Two policemen in uniform, one on either side, jerked Jack to his feet. In front of him was a middle aged policeman also in uniform, a peaked cap over a pink, shaven face. Others in uniform were standing back watching.

'Who are you?' barked the senior officer.

'Jack. Jack Bell. Just a builder,' exclaimed Jack, rolling his shoulders. 'I'm one of the good guys. What do you do to criminals?'

'I ask the questions,' said the police officer sternly. 'Don't cheek me.'

'I'm not cheeking,' said Jack. 'I was forced to come out here. That bastard in the house said if I'm not back in five minutes, he'd shoot one of us.'

The policeman looked to the others, plainly considering the truth or otherwise.

'You'd better tell us what's going on,' he said.

'Can you take these cuffs off? They're cutting into my wrists. I'm not going anywhere.'

'Get them off,' said the top cop. 'And if you've only got five minutes... you'd better get talking.'

As he began, Jack could feel the handcuffs coming off.

'I'm a builder, Jack Bell,' he rambled on, too scared, too excited, the words almost running away with him. 'You've got my cards there, that's my van over across the road. See, Jack of All Trades. I've been working on the house the last few days, doing repairs. And this morning, I just walked into this man with a gun. Anton...'

'Anton who?'

'I don't know his second name,' said Jack. 'There's...' he did a quick count in his head, 'seven of us. Anton has the gun. There's four hostages, including me. There's Mr Choudhury and his daughter Amina from 74.' He pointed out the Choudhury house. 'And there's Tosh, who's badly hurt. And that's another thing, Anton says bring a doctor. He says back off or he'll start killing us.' Jack was gasping as if he'd just finished a race. 'I've got to get back or he said he'd shoot Jan.'

'Why Jan?'

'He doesn't like her. She lives next door. There.' Jack pointed out her house. He was sweating, his heart thumping as he pulled at his collar to let air into his chest. He gazed at the cops, all staring at him. Were they taking it in? 'Anton's really jumpy,' he went, gesticulating. 'All these cars and guns are spooking him. He wants you out of sight. He wants a doctor for Tosh. I've got to get back in there or he'll start killing us. Please. You've got to believe me or he'll shoot Jan any minute.'

'OK, Jack. Calm down. I more or less get the picture. I believe you are who you say you are. With your overalls, that van, your cards. So tell this Anton, we'll back off and

154

we'll get a doctor.' He tapped Jack on the shoulder, avuncularly. 'Sorry about the roughing up, but we had no idea who you were.'

Jack waved his hands. 'And I have no idea who is going to kill me, that nutter or you lot.'

'It won't be us. I can assure you that. We're used to hostage situations. I'm Chief Inspector George Barker. I'll get these cars further up the road, our weapons out of sight. You'd best get back inside.'

'The last place I want to be.'

Jack hesitated, looking at the police and the cars. This was safety now. He'd won over the cops and now had to go back in the house. He could decide to stay here. Stay and live. But Anton had said he'd shoot Jan. In five minutes. They must be almost up.

'I'd better go in,' he said.

'Good luck, Jack.' The Chief Inspector patted him on the shoulder again.

He strode quickly across the road, had he been too long? Back up the path and into the house. He closed the front door after him. His lips were dry, sweat dripping down his back, legs hollow, he could barely command them to walk into the long room. But flight was not a possibility any longer. He was back here again, a willing victim.

'What was all that about?' exclaimed Anton as Jack came into the room. He was wiping his face with a sponge, his cheeks dripping, half brown, half white, his long hair wet.

'I had a hard time with the cops,' said Jack.

'I saw,' said Anton with a wry smile. 'They duffed you up.'

'They threw me to the ground, put cuffs on me. There was this Chief Inspector. I managed to persuade him that I was just the messenger...'

'And did you get through to him the situation here?' All the time, the gun pointing to Jack's chest.

'I told him you wanted the cops out of sight,' he said. 'They agreed to back off. I told them that you wanted a doctor. They said one would be coming.'

'Well done, Jack.' He slapped him on the shoulder, almost chummy, not that different from the Chief Inspector. 'You get two house points. You can join the others.'

Jack went to the rear of the room where the other hostages were sitting in a line against the wall, like naughty school children, forbidden to move or speak. He took a place at the end, next to Amina.

Chapter 28

The siege was settling down. The police knew the score. Their cars had withdrawn. How far couldn't be seen from the house, but less visually threatening. Anton had told Susie to lock the back door. So an easy escape route was blocked. They sat playing with their hands and faces, not allowed to communicate with each other. Anton kept looking through the curtains and seemed satisfied at the actions of the police. Jack noted that he made up his rules as he needed them. It was toilet needs forcing the next one. Aklis had to go. Anton said they were in pairs, each responsible for the other. He'd allow one of the pair to go to the toilet. If that one attempted escape, successful or otherwise, his partner would get shot. Jack was partnered with Jan, Amina with her father.

Aklis went to the toilet to test the scheme. The smallest room was along the hallway, near the back door. Jack knew it, having inspected it the other day, and knew too that Aklis could climb out of the window to the patio. So would Aklis come back from his visit? The way he'd treated his daughter certainly put it in doubt. But leaving her to be shot? That would be cowardly and dishonourable. But then Aklis could make up his reasons, if he chose. He had dropped so low in Jack's esteem.

They waited anxiously. Jack wondered whether Aklis, on his own, sitting on the toilet, was considering escaping. The door was locked, the window option obvious. It wouldn't be difficult. A ground floor window, out on to the patio. You didn't need to be an athlete. In next to no time, he could be back in his own house and then out with the police, telling of his brave escape, while his daughter was being shot.

But dead daughters are not marriageable.

Aklis returned and Jan went off. This was awful, this one by one test. His life on the line. He'd only known her two days. This was her chance to get out. She could justify it. It wasn't as if she were doing the killing. She was simply escaping from a place of terror. But then she owed him one. He'd come back from the police when he could've stayed with them and washed his hands of those inside.

She came back, and Amina went off. He'd be surprised if she tried to escape. Admittedly, her father had locked her up, but there was strong parental respect in Muslim households. More than Aklis deserved, but he didn't believe Amina would abandon him. All this was risky for Anton, but then Anton didn't have a lot of choice. There was only one of him. He couldn't go to the toilet with them. And Susie was occupied with Tosh, though he doubted she could be much help to the injured anarchist, beyond washing his face and holding his hand.

Amina returned, and Jack went to the toilet. Down the hallway, right at the end. The back door was locked, he noted, as well as bolted top and bottom. He locked himself in the toilet and breathed again, in spite of the smells of the recent users. It was the first place in half an hour where no one had held a gun on him.

He dropped his trousers. Freedom. How on earth were they to get out of this one? Somehow, Anton had to be convinced that what he was doing was futile. He couldn't escape. Couldn't get a plane to Cuba, or wherever was the latest refuge. Though he doubted there was one any longer.

The gunman had nowhere to go. Surely he realised that? Either he was just playing things out for as long as possible. Or, the more scary possibility, he was going to die fighting. If it came to that, who knows who would go down with him. Jack considered the possibility of jumping Anton. And considered the possibility of being shot in the attempt.

Toilet thoughts. He often had his best ideas in this space. He used the last scraps of toilet roll. Civilisation was stripping away.

And then returned to the room. Anton was pissing into a washing-up bowl. Having finished and done up his flies, he ordered Amina to empty it. She left with the bowl and came back a minute or so later.

'There's no toilet paper,' she said, 'and no soap either.'

'Thanks for that,' said Anton. 'We do need a few things. I'm in the middle of making a list.'

There was a ring on the bell. No one moved. Who the hell would come to a siege house? Susie rushed to the window.

'It's the doctor,' she cried.

Chapter 29

Dr Akira left the siege house and went to the police, behind their barricade of cars which had retreated down the road as requested. It was a relief to be out, though she'd worked in war zones for MSF. She hated guns, having seen too much of the damage they caused to the human body. Besides, a man holding a gun on her might sharpen her thinking when it came to self-preservation but wasn't necessarily good for her diagnosis. This, though, had been easy enough.

She was a youngish Asian woman, mid 30s, dressed in sensible, informal clothing: an outdoor, short coat over a green sweater and black trousers, with flat shoes. The police cars were about fifty yards away from the house, on either side. The road was blocked at either end by police; she'd been allowed in as she was expected, but other vehicles were ordered to turn round.

The Chief Inspector was drinking a coffee from a disposable cup as she approached.

'Would you like a hot drink, doctor?' he asked.

She waved it away. 'No, thank you.'

'What's the situation in there?'

'Grim,' she said. 'The young man has lost an enormous amount of blood. His chances are poor.'

'Did you tell them that?'

'No. There's the man with the gun...'

'Anton, I think his name is.'

'I told him that if the patient's life was to be saved then an ambulance must be called immediately. He didn't like that. And then this young woman was yelling at him. I think she was the patient's girlfriend. He yelled back at her. It was all going on over my head, back and forth. I felt like a kid in a family row...'

'What were they saying?'

'She was yelling – you shot him and now you won't allow an ambulance. That sort of stuff. He yells at her that their only chance of escape is to stick together. She screamed at him: you can't escape if you're dead.' Dr Akira gave a half smile. 'More or less. The gist of it, anyway.' She scratched her chin. 'Their row gave me the chance to look around. There were four hostages sitting down against the wall. Not talking. There was a middle aged Asian man in a white shirt and black trousers, a young Asian woman in salwar kameez, a youngish man in overalls and a youngish woman in jeans and sweatshirt.'

'Good observation,' said the Chief Inspector. 'What's happening about the ambulance?'

'The young woman got her way,' she said, 'I've called them. They should be here shortly. But frankly, I wouldn't bet on his survival. I wasn't much help. All I could do was clean him up and give him morphine.'

'It was brave of you to go in, doctor.'

She waved his thanks away. 'I never felt in any real danger. But the hostages...' She stopped to collect her thoughts. 'It was like being back in the Middle East. He treated them like the enemy. And enemy lives don't matter.'

The Chief Inspector thanked her for her observations, and she left. She had confirmed what the builder had said about the people inside the house. He had wondered whether he'd believed him too readily. If he might have been part of the gang. So the builder could be trusted. That was a relief. There were a lot of people watching this operation. One didn't want to appear the village idiot.

So a lone gunman, four hostages, a wounded man and his girlfriend. The wounded man was part of the bank raid; he knew that from CCTV footage, but not the girlfriend's part. A minor part perhaps, or even totally innocent. Not one to worry about. The man with the gun was the big concern. Who the hell was he? Anton, a first name wasn't much to go on. Leader of a bunch of incompetents. A bungled robbery, the car so easily identifiable outside the house, not five minutes away. That didn't make him less dangerous, of course. Perhaps more so.

Susie wiped Tosh's brow with a damp sponge. She was kneeling beside him as he lay flat out on a sleeping bag, a roll of clothing under his head. The sleeping bag was soaked in blood.

'They've called the ambulance, sweetheart.'

'We were stupid,' he said weakly. He clutched her hand with both of his. 'Why did I go along with it?'

'They'll get you to hospital, Tosh. And you'll be alright. You won't be in prison long. Anton has the gun. He did all the shooting. I'll wait for you. I'll come and visit you.'

'The pain's gone,' said Tosh. 'That injection the doctor gave me worked.' He tried a smile and coughed.

She rubbed his chest, a tear rolling down her cheek. 'My darling, my darling. Please live.'

'Anton should give himself up,' he said, phlegm almost blocking his throat. 'He can't shoot the world. Oh dear, what a mess we made.' He moaned and closed his eyes.

She wiped his forehead, feeling utterly useless as he dropped into sleep. It had gone so wrong. What was she doing here? Anton was a loud-mouthed loser. They were all losers. She hoped he wouldn't shoot anyone else. They didn't deserve it. Or who would be left in the world if Anton were in control? A death sentence to anyone not as pure as he was. Dear Tosh. He was really so gentle. They had come here together. What was he doing on bank raids? She kissed his forehead.

'Sleep, my darling, sleep. Let your body heal.'

She almost prayed. She didn't believe in God. Could you have God and bullets in the same world? God and the hydrogen bomb. God with half the world starving... Why should He lift a finger to save Tosh? Why save anyone? He'd let them drown by the hundred thousand in the tsunami. None of it made sense.

'Dear God, save him. He's young. So talented. He meant no harm. Give him a chance to make up for it.'

Anton was standing over Jack. His face was more or less wiped clean, with just a little brown round the eyes. He said, 'I've made up a list. You're to go outside again. Tell them what I want. Five minutes, no more. You know the rules. Or Jan gets it.'

Jack nodded his agreement. The gun didn't allow otherwise.

'Which of these phones is yours?' Anton held out a box with three phones that he'd taken off them earlier.

'That one,' said Jack, pointing out his own.

'Take it with you,' said Anton. 'I want to be in phone communication with them. Instead of depending on you, nice guy that you are. Take your phone. And get their number. I might need to talk directly with the chief.'

Jack took it, and the list. He headed out of the house. He was weary, dry; he'd had nothing to drink since breakfast. Amina had asked for water and it had been refused. Not a good sign for their longevity.

The sun was high in the sky, though this side of the road was in shadow. The police cars were about fifty yards away in both directions. He didn't know which way to go. He hesitated in the middle of the road, looking one way and then the other.

'This way, Jack,' called a voice.

Jack saw someone waving behind the cars on his left hand side. He headed that way. Behind the barricade of vehicles was a group of policemen including Chief Inspector

George Barker. This time, he had a friendlier welcome.

'How's it going, Jack?'

'When it's not boring, it's scary, when it's not scary, it's boring. I don't know what he plans to do with us,' he said wearily.

'We've got a hostage negotiator coming,' said Barker. 'So we need to be able to communicate directly with Anton.'

'He wants that too,' said Jack. 'He gave me my phone to swap numbers with you.'

'Let's do that.'

'Yep. I've only five minutes again.'

They swapped numbers. The Chief Inspector rang Jack's to test they worked. It rang.

'We are in communication,' said Barker. 'A step forward, I hope.'

'I've got a list for you,' said Jack. He took it out of his overalls and handed it over.

Barker perused the list. 'Let me see. Salted peanuts, biscuits, coke, crisps. He likes prawn cocktail. Well, well. I wonder what our hostage negotiator will make of that. Soap, toilet rolls. A television set. He must be missing the afternoon antique shows.'

'Can I have a drink of water?' said Jack.

'Sorry,' said Barker. 'How remiss of me.' He waved a hand. 'A bottle of water for Jack here.'

The water came, the top removed for him. He drank it all, the inspector watching as he sank the 500 ml.

'Is he not allowing you water?'

'I was going to fill up at the next toilet break. But no. Amina asked and he yelled at her for speaking without him speaking first.' He half grinned. 'Though I doubt we'll die of thirst.'

'Tell him his list is being attended to.'

Jack's phone rang. He looked at it.

'It's my ex,' he said. 'Can I answer it?'

'Yes, tell her not to use this line again.'

'Hello, Alison.'

'Jack, can you have Mia for tonight?'

'I'd love to,' he said. 'But I'm a hostage...'

'You're joking.'

'I'm not. And you mustn't use this line again. The police need it.'

'Not the Forest Gate siege? It's all over TV and radio.'

'The very same. Must ring off or I'll be in trouble. Please don't ring me back.'

He rang off. Exhausted with the short call.

'I'd better get back to the house.'

The Chief Inspector gripped his arm. 'We are doing all we can, Jack. I assure you. But I know from experience not to rush in. Anton needs to realise he has no choice but surrender.'

'Let's hope he's got that much sense.'

Jack left the comfort of the police barricade. Barker watched him go back along the road and then turn into the house. An expensive operation, this, but finance was not a problem. He'd had a phone call from the Commissioner. Asking what was being done, offering help. Watching. TV was here. He must get this right, for everyone's benefit, for his future.

He needed to hurry along the hostage negotiator. Barker looked again at the list he was holding in his hand, smiled wryly at the inclusion of a TV set, then idly turned the page over. It was a leaflet for a factory picket. He read it, the usual wild far left rant. From Red Anger.

That was worth chasing up. All this undercover stuff the police did on the far left. They must have something on Red Anger. Or why bother?

Chapter 30

Mrs Choudhury went to the library on Woodgrange Road, not to get a book out but to see her daughter, Inaya, who worked there as an assistant librarian. There were two in charge of the library today. The other woman was senior and when Mrs Choudhury told her that she must talk to Inaya as the police had evacuated their house because of the situation next door, she at once assented to Inaya talking privately with her mother.

Inaya took her mother to an isolated section of the library. They sat close together and spoke quietly.

Inaya said, 'This road has gone mad today. Police everywhere. The Halifax Bank was raided in broad daylight. Can you believe it? One of our cleaners was there. She was hysterical when she came in. She said the doors were locked and they all had to lie on the ground face down. There were two robbers, one of them going crazy, shooting everywhere. 'Where's the money!' he kept screaming. 'You must have more than this!' A security guard was shot, other people injured, the other robber too. It was a mad house, she said. And they got hardly anything. Once they'd gone, the police were there in no time. In the library, we wondered what was going on out there. Sirens sounding. What a racket! I went out to have a look. Police cars, ambulances everywhere. It's still a crime scene, that section of the road.' She stopped, to allow her words to catch up with her thoughts. 'You just don't expect it here. In films, but not on your own high street.'

Her mother said, 'I don't know what's happening to Forest Gate. So much crime these days. Drugs and shootings. That's why I'm here. We've had to move out of our house temporarily. The police came to our door. They said there's a man next door with a gun holding hostages and we must leave until it's over.'

Inaya's hands came to her cheeks. 'Next door! Those squatters. With a gun! How awful. What's going on today?'

'Well you may ask. Our road is full of police cars,' said Mrs Choudhury. 'Some of the police have guns. And we must leave. I don't know for how long. They couldn't tell me. I asked and the policeman said, maybe a few hours, maybe a few days. Can you believe that?' She shook her head in disbelief. 'A few days outside our house.'

'Who are the hostages?' said Inaya.

She shrugged. 'I don't know. What goes on in that house is a total mystery to me. All I know is that there's a dangerous man in there – and we can't go home until the police have got him.'

'What a day!' exclaimed Inaya. 'It's happening all round us. A bank robbery and a man holding hostages... '

'I couldn't contact your father,' exclaimed Mrs Choudhury. 'I was vacuuming the downstairs. I didn't hear him go out. And his phone is off. So he has no idea what is going on.'

'He always turns his phone off,' said Inaya. 'And then forgets about it.'

'Well, I told the police to tell him that we've gone to my sister in Ilford. Your granny has already gone in a taxi. I wish I could contact your father.'

'Don't worry,' said Inaya. 'Daddy will phone us when he comes home, I'm sure.' She leaned in closer and said more quietly, 'What about Amina?'

'That's strange too,' exclaimed her mother. 'You know we locked her in her room?'

'How could I not know? She was banging and yelling... You and Daddy were shouting at her.'

'I wasn't sure about locking her in, but it was your

father's idea. He said it would help her see sense.' She looked about to make sure no one could hear her family business, before continuing. 'But she's escaped.'

'How could she escape?'

'I unlocked her room after the police had come, and she wasn't there. The window was cut.'

'What do you mean it was cut?'

'I mean a square piece was cut out of the glass. And outside, in the garden was a ladder...'

'The builder!' exclaimed Inaya. 'Jack. It must be him. He will have taken her to Jan's.'

'Oh, that interfering woman!' hissed Mrs Choudhury. 'Well, I'm not going there. Your father must deal with it.' She flapped her hands. 'Oh, this dreadful business.' She sighed deeply. 'Wasif Khan wants to know her answer. We had to tell him that Amina was considering his offer most favourably but wanted another day to think about it.'

They were quiet for a while, the situation in the road and next door and their own situation seemed to be overlapping. Chaos. It was fitting, thought Inaya, that their road should be full of police. And then she had a thought.

She said, 'If we've been evacuated, Mummy, then Jan, on the other side, will have been evacuated too.'

'I never thought of that,' said Mrs Choudhury pressing her fingers against her lips. 'Amina will have gone with her. Wherever that may be.' She turned to her daughter, her voice rising. 'I can see it; we are heading for disaster. This marriage with Wasif Khan, which should have been our salvation, won't happen. The house will be sold over our heads.'

Inaya held her mother's hand. 'Not so loud, Mummy, please.'

'Sorry, sorry.' She flapped her hands. 'If only your father would answer his phone. That man drives me mad.'

'It was his get-rich-quick scheming that got us into trouble in the first place.'

'Then he must get us out of it.' And she was weeping.

Inaya hugged her, too aware that others were looking at them. They rocked together, the two women. She'd been so glad to get out of the house that morning, all the fuss of the night before, her sister locked in, her mother and father so angry. There'd been all that yelling and recrimination when she'd got back with Amina. She'd slept badly, wondering if she should have left Amina at Jan's and not brought her home. Would Amina ever forgive her? And now she was gone. It shouldn't be a surprise, except it was. Her sister, her enemy. And now no one could go back to the house because of a man with a gun next door.

How much longer would she be able to call it next door?

Her mother wiped her eyes. 'It's no good me crying. That helps nobody. I don't know what we'll do. I don't know who's worse, your father or Amina.' She sniffed. 'I shall get the bus to Ilford. If the situation is the same, then you come to your auntie's after work. Join me and Granny.' She shook her hands in frustration. 'I don't know what I'm going to say to your auntie.'

Chapter 31

Lunch would be over by now at school, thought Amina. That's where she should be by rights. Taking the children out, one at a time, for special reading. She thought of some of the children; those she could help and those who were simply befuddled. Some children raced away with reading, some couldn't get started. She'd like to know about the latest methods, the computer programs and techniques. Fat chance, for a lowly teaching assistant. She knew you had to get children to a point where they could get on to the reading schemes, then read themselves up the ladder. It was that beginning that was so crucial. The deciphering and remembering of words, making the connections and not simply guessing. At times, she felt helpless with a struggling child. She hated that. There must be strategies she'd never even thought about.

All very well, these thoughts, but her father had different ideas for her. Marriage to Wasif Khan, to get him out of the hole he'd dug for himself. Or rather dug for the family. Her role was to sacrifice herself for them. She had supposed they'd got beyond that traditional female role, the virtual enslavement of women, staying in the house, covering up completely when they went out, marry who we say, all that bygone tradition. Her family were enlightened. Past tense. They'd lost their enlightenment with Daddy's money.

She'd hardly slept last night, spending her time planning how to escape. The easy way out was to pretend to agree with her parents, so they'd free her. And then run away. The problem was where to go. She'd heard of refuges for battered women. Was she a battered woman? The way she'd been pushed around last night, she must fit the description.

So suppose she went to a refuge? The family house

would be lost and they'd blame her for the rest of their lives. Because you couldn't blame Daddy. Oh no. Not the one who caused it, but the one who wouldn't marry an old man.

Did they even know that Wasif Khan would buy the house? Amina suspected they hadn't asked him yet. That would be sprung on him after the marriage. How to endear a new wife to a husband! Suppose he said no. Then she'd have married him for no advantage to her family, lost all chance of personal ambition, or marrying for love to someone her own age.

Strangely, she wasn't so affected by being a hostage. A little scared but, in a way, her life was in limbo anyway. She'd been a captive last night, and had made her escape this morning. Free for perhaps a minute. And back to jail.

At least this time, she wasn't the prime victim. Anton had questioned her at one point. He had gone from one to the other, trying to catch them out. She had her sins, but they were more than supplanted by her good points. She had told him that she was a teaching assistant. He approved. She said she wanted to be a teacher. 'In a state school?' he shot back. 'Of course,' she'd said. 'I want to specialise in reading. Too many children are leaving school virtually illiterate. That's wrong.' And he'd agreed with her, amazingly, giving some complicated economic argument she couldn't really follow, but she nodded in assent, as one does when a man holds a gun on you.

If the shooting started, it would be Jan that got it. Anton hated her for being rich and owning a big house. Actually, Amina knew, Jan owned two big houses. Her father when questioned said he was virtually bankrupt. That didn't go down well with Anton. As quite obviously, her father wanted to be a millionaire but just wasn't very good at it. Though he was getting punished for his ineptitude. A point or two for that. No one had brought up Wasif Khan, the fairy godmother in the wings.

Jack had done alright in the questioning. Well, he was a worker. Blessed be thy name. Amina had picked that up quickly. Anton loved workers. She was the third to be questioned, after Jack, so she'd an advantage. Struggling workers were the best of all. So Jack who had hardly two pennies to rub together was on his way to heaven. Strange way of looking at things. And Jan? Well, Amina thought, Jan just hadn't worked out the game. It was no good saying you earned £140,000 last year, which is what she had said. She could have stripped a hundred thou off that. But then, maybe the rest wouldn't hold water. Owning a big house. She'd had to admit that she'd inherited it. Anton had missed a trick there in not asking her where she'd lived before. A house she owned out in Essex somewhere, which she now let. But it hardly mattered, she was damned enough.

Amina decided that if the shooting started that Jan would be the first to go. Then her father. After that it was iffy, between her and Jack. Jack was better workwise but she was an ethnic minority which upped her score.

Unless she had it all wrong. And it would be random. Scattered shooting. Then it would come down to how quickly the police got in. And the poor girl might get it too. Amina had gathered that her boyfriend had died. He was obviously in a bad way when they'd first arrived, not that she could see that well from where she was but there was a lot of blood. It stained the girl's clothes. And she surmised, things were not going well from the doctor's words and the girl's tears. The ambulance had come but it had been too late for him. They'd covered him up, so that was clear enough; they were taking away a corpse. She would have liked to have put her arms round the girl. Comforted her. Though really, that was hardly possible. Her boyfriend had died in front of her. Amina had picked up, when the girl and Anton were yelling at each other, that Anton had accidentally shot him during a bank raid. Maybe shot others, that wasn't clear.

How did the girl fit in? She wasn't at the robbery, Amina gathered. But she wasn't a hostage, so what was she? A friend of Anton's, no, hardly that either. Not the way she shouted and screamed at him. The remarkable thing was that he allowed it.

She had a lot to think about, which was just as well, as she had lots of time. Food had come and a television. And toilet rolls, thank goodness. They didn't get any of the food. Anton offered it to the girl, but she wasn't interested, so he had a big cardboard box all for himself. Greedy pig. Jack had set up the television for him. A 40-inch flat screen thing. Once working, Anton had put it on the BBC News channel and left it on mute until they had come up. Weird to see the house, all the police on the street outside. There were witnesses from the bank robbery on Woodgrange. If she survived, most likely she would be interviewed.

It was odd sitting next to her father all this time and not able to talk to him. Would he blame her for their captivity? Probably. If she hadn't tried to escape, he would yell at her, then he wouldn't have had to chase after her and get made a hostage. All her fault. Like the house. And really, when it came down to it, if she'd simply said yes to Wasif Khan, like a dutiful daughter, all would be sweetness and light. So, maybe, just as well she couldn't speak to him. She could have touched his hand, but what would that say to him? That she forgave him, when she most certainly hadn't.

Chapter 32

When Helen Fisher, the school secretary, came in with a file, Alison was watching the small TV up on the shelf in her office.

'I'm surprised you've got time to watch that,' said Helen.

'I haven't. It's the siege in Forest Gate. My ex-husband is caught up in it.'

'What, Mia's dad? What's his name...' she flicked her fingers.

'Jack. He's one of the hostages.'

'Oh my God!' Helen's hands went to her face. 'Is he really? They killed someone in a bank or something.'

'I phoned him about an hour ago,' said Alison, 'and he told me I had to get off the line as this was the phone the gunman was using...' She gave a half laugh, 'I wanted him to look after Mia tonight.'

'Well, he's got a good excuse not to.' She realised what she had said and patted Alison on the back. 'I am sorry. It's serious, isn't it?'

'The news says the gunman has four or five hostages. They're unsure about the exact number. He's already killed a security guard at the bank, and wounded some others. The house is surrounded by cops. Look.' She indicated the TV pictures which showed the police on the street, and then the back gardens where there were also armed police. 'He can't possibly escape.'

'Why doesn't he just give himself up?'

'Killers don't think like me and you, Helen.' The subject on the TV switched, and she turned it off with the remote. 'He does get into some straits, my ex. But I am quite fond of him in spite of the terrible time he gave me. I don't want him shot.'

'You'd lose a child minder. Oh, I am sorry, Alison. It's the way I deal with these things. I get silly. Make jokes. And there's these hostages in a house with a mad gunman...'

Helen was going through a filing cabinet and picking out files, distracted, taking out the wrong ones and putting them back.

Alison looked at her wall clock. 'I've got year 3 awards assembly in ten minutes.' She was undecided what to do. She couldn't do anything for Jack, but was worried for him. She looked about her office. It was roomy and helped her to feel like a Head when she had visitors. It looked out onto a small garden where in fine weather teachers ate their lunch. There was a photograph of Mia on her desk, and on the wall a print of Renoir's Umbrellas. Mia liked it, especially the little girl with the hoop and her big sister with flowers in her hat.

'I've put an offer on a house in that area,' mused Alison.

'I'm sure bank robberies and hostage-takings are only occasional,' said Helen, closing the filing cabinet.

'These things come out of the blue,' said Alison. 'He could be dead tomorrow. Poof, like that. I really mustn't say such things, but you can't help thinking it. It's hard to concentrate.'

'Of course,' said Helen, 'it's why it's so dreadful. You can't help putting yourself in their shoes.'

'I do hope he'll be OK.' She was about to turn the TV back on. 'No, no. I must be head teacher. Have you got the agenda for the Governors' meeting? I'll have a quick perusal before the assembly.'

Chapter 33

'How do you do, Chief Inspector. I'm Beryl Greene. Your hostage negotiator.'

He shook her hand. She was a middle-aged woman, tall and slim, her light hair short and speckled. She wore a check dress suit.

'What do you think?' said Barker, not one for small talk.

'I've had a briefing and seen the bank CCTV footage. That's disturbing. His shooting spree lasted no more than twenty seconds, and in that time he'd killed the security guard, wounded his colleague and five others.'

'His colleague has died,' said Barker. 'The ambulance took him away half an hour ago.'

'He wasn't involved in the shooting. It was all Anton,' she said. 'Curious name. Eastern European.'

'We are trying to find out more about him,' said Barker. 'We think he might belong to an anarchist group called Red Anger. I'm awaiting a report.'

'The bank footage shows Anton is very touchy. His body language quite explosive,' she said. 'Once he'd found out the money hadn't come, he went crazy. So if we want to keep the hostages alive, we mustn't thwart him in any way.'

'I've been playing it low key,' said Barker. 'I've pulled everyone back, out of sight. And anything he wants I've given to him. Even a TV set.'

Beryl laughed. 'He wants to watch his fifteen minutes of fame.'

'I'm considering getting into the house,' said Barker. 'Quietly. A surprise attack. There's a skylight on the back roof. We could get over the rooftops to it, without him knowing.'

'It's high risk,' she said. 'Should he find out, it could press his panic button – and he could shoot them all before you get to him.'

'Could be a disaster,' he agreed. 'But could be the only way. If we could get say three armed officers in... It would be useful to know the layout of the house. We think Anton and the hostages are all confined in the downstairs sitting room.'

'Would your officers know who to shoot at?'

'That's the problem,' said Barker. 'The CCTV pictures are poor. It appears they were wearing wigs and painted up...'

'They could either shoot the wrong people,' said Beryl. 'Or if he hears them coming, he could shoot the hostages before they get him. Could be a bloodbath.'

'We can't simply leave it to him,' said Barker. 'It's risky whatever we do.'

'Yes,' she agreed. 'We need to work on a couple of fronts. We must find out all we can about Anton.'

'I'll hurry them along.'

'Even partial information would be helpful. Are we in communication with him?'

'We have a phone line.'

'Then I want to speak to him, but we need to consider exactly what I say.'

Chapter 34

He was cold in his shirt sleeves, and hungry. The least of his troubles. If he'd simply let Amina go this morning, none of this would be happening. Well, not quite. She'd still be a hostage but he wouldn't. And he, himself, probably wouldn't have caught Amina anyway. She'd have got to Jan's. What would he have done then, break the door in? He was too impetuous. And now look where he was.

What a mess he'd made of everything. His business dealings. Oh, why hadn't he stopped with one shop! It's the only one profitable. Anton had called him greedy, and Anton was right. You are greedy if you go for the big one and fail. No one called Wasif Khan greedy.

You aim to make a good marriage for your daughter. That means with someone who can keep her. Well, Wasif could do that in spades. But also, you want someone who would make her happy. That was one hundred per cent failure. And brought him here, with a crazy man with a gun.

It was Amina who deserved to be free. Not him. How could he imprison his own daughter? He'd been dwelling on that all morning. Those were the old ways. Total submission. Father is always right. Not this idiot. Call a fool a fool.

If he hadn't imprisoned her last night, then she would have gone back to Jan's with her clothing. He wouldn't be here, Amina wouldn't be here. He had chased her into the clutches of a gunman. Of course, he didn't know he was doing that.

No excuse.

He was still angry with her. Part of him was. He did want her to marry Wasif Khan. Of course, Wasif didn't know his potential father-in-law was in big financial trouble. He couldn't offload that on him and have any hope of pulling the marriage off. It would look so mercenary. As it was in fact, but the idea had been to get the marriage over with – and then spring it on him.

And suppose he then said no, as he had a perfect right to? Then Aklis would be a double fool. And a nasty one to boot. He'd sacrificed his daughter for nothing. That would make a good Arabian Nights tale: *The Foolish Father*.

He had considered suicide over the last few weeks. It was a sin. And would still leave his family in trouble. Leaving them alone to sort the mess out. To curse his name. But now he had another thought, one that might work and wouldn't condemn him. Suppose he went for Anton's gun. Of course, he wouldn't get it, and Anton would kill him.

Then he'd be a hero and his life insurance would pay up. It wouldn't in the case of suicide but for murder it would. It was a way. The insurance would cover quite a lot of his debt. It might mean the house was saved, the calculations were complicated, depending on the bank and his main creditor. They might be sympathetic to the plight of his widow and her daughters.

So how and when? He'd want Anton to be occupied, so it looked like he had a chance of succeeding, instead of a desperate lunge. He must pick his moment.

Amina was by his side. She had been all the time. He wanted to touch her hand, to say it's alright, my dear daughter, forgive me. I am going to do something that will put things right. But how might she read his touch? Perhaps she'd think he was using love as a compulsion, saying join the fold, do as you are bid and you will have my blessing again.

He kept his hand by his side.

The phone rang. Anton leapt up and pulled it out of his pocket. He held it outstretched to Jack.

'Answer it, builder. It might be one of your customers.'

Jack took the phone. Was that the phone number of the police? He couldn't remember.

'Hello,' he said cautiously.

'Hello,' said a woman. 'Am I speaking to Anton?'

'Are you the police?' he said.

'I am in a manner of speaking. I'm Beryl Greene, the hostage negotiator. Are you Anton?'

'I'm Jack, one of his hostages. I'll ask him if he wants to speak to you.' Jack took the phone from his ear. He said to Anton, 'There's a woman wants to speak to you. She's a hostage negotiator.'

'Tell her to get lost.'

Jack put the phone back to his ear and spoke into it. 'He said he doesn't want to speak to you.'

'I heard exactly what he said,' said Beryl. 'Ask him if there is anything he needs, if there is any way we can help him.'

Anton went to grab the phone off Jack, but before he got to it Aklis threw himself at him. Amina screamed. The others jerked back. Aklis got within clutching distance when Anton fired twice at him from point blank range.

Everyone froze. Jack was fearful Anton might shoot the rest of them. His reaction hung by a hair. Anton stepped back, away from the prone body of Aklis, his arm still stretched out.

'What's going on in there?' exclaimed Beryl. 'Hello?'

'Aklis Choudhury tried to get the gun from Anton,' said Jack, still numb. 'And Anton shot him.'

'Tell the cow it was his own fault,' hissed Anton, waving the gun at Jack.

'Anton says it was Choudhury's own fault,' said Jack. His mouth was dry, he was watching the shaky gun in Anton's hand. 'He's not threatening the rest of us,' he said. Anton nodded at him. 'We're not in any danger.'

Anton grabbed the phone from Jack, than stepped quickly back. 'The nutter charged at me,' he yelled into it. 'What did he expect?'

'Is he alive?' said Beryl.

'How should I know?'

'Can I phone for an ambulance?' she asked.

'Do whatever you want.' He closed the call and strode across the room to the window, snarling.

Amina went to her father. She knelt by his side, she licked the back of her hand and put it close to his mouth. She held it there for a while.

'He's still breathing,' she said.

Chapter 35

Beryl and CI Barker were watching the progress of the paramedics with their stretcher. They had just come out of the house and were followed closely by Jack. The stretcher was heavy, and the bearers strained with the weight of it. Their ambulance was just outside the house, its back doors wide open. Once the stretcher was inside, one paramedic stayed with the patient and the other ran round the front to get in the driving seat. Within a few seconds, they were off, going slowly to get free of the police barricade. Barker waved them down. The vehicle stopped, the driver brought his window half down.

'How is he?' said Barker.

'Just about alive.'

'What are his chances?'

The driver pursed his lips. 'That's over my pay grade. Best get him straight to Intensive Care or he stands no chance.'

'Don't let me delay you.'

He waved the ambulance on. The window went up and the vehicle headed off. Once beyond the police cars, it sped off, siren blasting. Jack had stopped at Barker. Beryl Greene was with him.

'Five minutes,' said Jack, looking back to the house as if the gunman might come out to hasten him.

Barker nodded. He knew the drill. He indicated the woman by him. 'Beryl Greene, negotiator.'

'We spoke on the phone,' said Jack.

'Yes, we did. Pleased to meet you, Jack.'

'What does he want this time?' said Barker.

'He wants to assure you that it wasn't his fault.'

Barker smiled wryly. 'Thousands wouldn't agree.'

'Me neither,' said Jack. 'But all I can say is that Aklis made a lunge at him. Presumably to get the gun. At the time, Anton was listening to me on the phone and Aklis thought he had a chance.' Jack shrugged. 'Mad. But brave.'

'What's Anton done since?' asked Beryl.

'He stomped around swearing for a few minutes,' Jack gave a half laugh, 'then, can you believe it? gave us all a can of coke, a bag of crisps and two chocolate biscuits.'

'That's good,' said Beryl. 'He's calmed down. Feels guilty. And it shows he wants to live. At least for the time being.'

'So, do you feel in danger, Jack?' said Barker.

'Yes,' he said. 'Eight out of ten on the scale. Down from nine after the shooting.'

'Why did he send you out?' enquired Beryl, 'instead of talking to us on the phone.'

'He says he's no good on the phone.' Jack shrugged. 'For some reason, he trusts me. I've got what he wanted each time I've come out. But I'm worried about Jan. She's number one on his hit list. He wasn't going to give her coke and crisps – but Susie persuaded him to.'

'What's wrong with Jan?' said Beryl.

'She's a filthy capitalist bitch – to quote his more pleasant phrases.'

Barker looked at Beryl. 'I'm sure that's Red Anger-speak,' he said. Then scratched his lower cheek. 'I want to sound you out on something. You know the building?'

'Inside and out. I've been working there for a couple of days.'

'What's the chances of getting in through the back skylight? Wait a mo'.' He brought out a small hand held recorder. 'I'm going to record this.' He pressed a button. 'It's on now. So how would you get to Anton and the hostages through the skylight, Jack?'

Jack thought for a moment, Barker was holding the

recorder close to Jack's mouth. 'You go across the roofs from the house next door, the Choudhurys' place. They'll need a double extension ladder to get up there, and then a roof ladder to get up to the ridge. Then shuffle along the ridge with the roof ladder. Down to the skylight. They'll have to break the glass. But it might just push out as I only put it in this morning. If it doesn't, use a glass cutter, and a suction plunger to stop it falling inwards, so it can't be heard from downstairs. Then you're in the loft. There's a trapdoor to the bathroom. I'd bring a small ladder along or he might hear you drop to the floor. Then out of the bathroom, down the stairs, it's carpeted, and we are first on the right at the bottom, nearest to the front door.'

'What's Anton look like?'

'He's the only guy who's not me. There's three women: Susie, Jan and Amina. And me. Anton's got long, dark brown hair to his shoulders. He's short, maybe five feet four and skinny. He's wearing jeans and a green T-shirt. Tell them not to shoot the guy in overalls.' He looked at them anxiously. 'And tell them to keep quiet, or we're goners. No mad rushes. I've got to get back now. What shall I tell him?'

'That we understand why he had to do it,' said Beryl. 'And it's business as usual.'

'Ask him what he wants for dinner,' said Barker wryly.

Jack gave them a wave and headed back. His stomach was churning. The police were coming in. There'd be bullets everywhere. He wasn't sure who he was more afraid of, Anton or the cops.

Chapter 36

He kept going out to the cops. That was the third time Anton had sent him. And each time, Jan wondered whether Jack would come back. So cunning of Anton to partner them. He probably knew and enjoyed how much she suffered in the waiting. She wasn't wearing her watch, having set out first thing to do building work. How long five minutes can be! Every time he left the house, she thought: he's safe out there, among the cops – why should he return? What does he owe me? Secure, away from Anton's watching gun. She wondered if she would come back, if she'd got the chance to go out there. What did she owe Jack? She'd only known him just over two days. So they'd slept together. Never a reason to give up your life. She'd slept with her husband for over seven years, and would happily abandon him to a gunman.

Not that it would have lasted with Jack, anyway. He was barely making a living. She hadn't realised. If they ever lived together, she'd be keeping him, just like her husband. Never that again. The kept man lounging around, leeching off her money, while she drew animal builders. The irony. Anton was watching again. She shivered; he had the cruellest face, a sharp, bony structure, chipped teeth. Tosh could have captured it so well, the essence of nastiness. It must be five minutes, at least. If only the bastard didn't stare. He hated her so much for owning a large house, for making a good living. He'd told her she took the bread out of poor people's mouths. He was a stew of hatreds, each meaty chunk was her sin. Anton was looking at his watch, and coming over. Jack, please come back. Don't you dare abandon me! I have everything to live for.

Jack returned in a rush, slamming the front door. Anton pointed to his watch as he came into the room. Jack apologised and told him that he'd had a long conversation with the police, persuading them that Anton had had no choice with Aklis. He had got through to them, but it had taken time, all the explanation. He apologised again, saying everything was alright. And Anton waved him back to his place along the wall with the others.

Jack sat down with relief. He'd been out probably more than five minutes. A minute or so over, maybe. He was concerned that having shot once and got away with it, Anton would find it easier to do it again. He must be kept calm, especially with the cops coming in. They wouldn't be that long, he figured. All the gear was readily available. Any builder, himself included, could supply the ladders and anything else. They must have had training at getting into places without noise, surely? He'd seen them in the movies smashing down doors and screaming *Police!* whereas this was a tiptoes exercise.

From the beginning, he'd been scared, but now knowing what the police were about to do, there was a level of terror he could barely deal with. Bullets would be flying, he had no doubt. And they were defenceless.

Keep cool, don't panic, hope.

Susie was squatting on the floor, where Tosh had been, as if he were still there. Her darling Tosh. They'd met on a picket line, outside a burger chain. And instantly clicked. He'd drawn a picture of her that day, interrupting himself from drawing the cops. How could he be dead when he was so alive in her? So kind, so generous. Both had abandoned their families. They were the new world. A world without hierarchies, where the rich didn't tread on the poor. A dream that had taken them to this East End squat, along with Anton and his wild schemes. She'd been enthralled by Red Anger. Its HQ in Bethnal Green. Their fury at the system. The group had a rage, they wanted to burn society down and build afresh from the ashes. Hooray! She and

Tosh were babes in the wood, wanting to be heroes in the movie of capitalism's collapse. Or was it the workers' triumph? Or was it silly men with guns in banks, who assured you nothing could go wrong, that it was all carefully planned, don't worry your daft head.

How he strutted about with his weapon, eating prawn cocktail crisps. She would never touch another one. And Coke, the epitome of capitalism. He pulled the ring off as if it was the pin of a grenade. That mad man, who'd shot her Tosh. It was an accident, he'd assured her, all Tosh's fault, for being in front of the gun when it fired. As if the gun were in charge. What was worse, him or her stupidities? She only knew, he mustn't kill again. He'd shot Aklis. Bam, bam. So quick. The pinhead, constipated with Marxist babble, playing with his remaining hostages like a cat with mice. It was obvious who his next victim would be. Jan, with those lovely tales. Susie had delighted in them, but all Anton saw was her money and her house. Tosh had known better. He'd tell Susie, you mustn't rub out art or all you have is blood and death. Her darling Tosh.

Anton joined his hostages, sitting down, leaning against the opposite wall to them. The box of depleting goodies by him. He was explaining himself for the umpteenth time.

'I am sorry about what happened,' said Anton. 'Believe me. But he threw himself at me. What on earth was I to do?'

None of those sitting opposite him answered. Anton had the gun in his lap, as if to show he meant them no harm. For now, at least.

'If he'd got the gun, he'd have shot me.' He grinned at them as if proud of his broken teeth. 'I expect you think that would have been a good thing, Jan.'

Jan was looking at the ground in front of her. She did not reply.

'I asked you a question, Jan.' His hand went round the handle of the gun.

She looked at him. 'What do you want me to say?'

'What you think.'

She didn't answer for a second but gave a weary sigh. Then said, 'You only did what was right.'

He passed the gun from hand to hand as if testing the weight. 'You are lying, Jan.'

'I am lying,' she said.

'So you agree with me?'

She screwed up her face as if a little lost. 'I agree with you.'

'Is that because you are a capitalist pig?'

'Yes.'

Jack knew her strategy was to agree with Anton whatever he said. What was the point of arguing with a gun?

Anton, perhaps tiring of his easy victim, turned to Amina and smiled brightly at her. 'What shall we do with the capitalist pig, Amina?'

She thought for a second, then said, 'Tax her.'

'Oh, Amina, isn't that somewhat feeble?'

'Yes,' she said, 'but it's what I think.'

Anton put his hand in the cardboard box by his side and took out a half opened packet of chocolate digestive biscuits. Slowly and deliberately, he removed the biscuits from the packet and placed them in a tidy column in front of him.

'For such a wussy answer, Amina, you deserve a chocolate biscuit.'

He took aim and flicked it at her as hard as he could. Amina brought her hands to her face as it struck her on the chest, relatively harmlessly.

'Lucky there's no coke left,' he hissed. 'It's you lackeys that protect the system.' He took up another biscuit, took aim, delighted at the way she protected herself with her arms. Then put it back down on the heap, and turned to Jack. 'How do you think this will end?'

'I don't know.'

'I think you have some idea. Try again.'

Jack thought for a few seconds. He didn't want to antagonise Anton, nor tell him what he really thought. He said, 'We could be dead, you could be dead, or anything between.'

'Try to be a little more precise, Jack.'

Anton was moving the gun from thigh to thigh, making Jack realise he was more agitated than he sounded.

'It depends on you,' Jack said. 'But your choices are limited.'

'How are they?'

He didn't want to answer, not knowing how much Anton had thought out for himself. Or what he wanted to hear. But had to say something.

'You know this place is surrounded?'

'I ask the questions,' said Anton. 'Have a chocolate digestive.'

He flicked one at Jack. Jack ducked and it hit the wall behind him. He straightened up. Anton was staring at him, waiting.

'There are lots of cops out front in the street,' said Jack. 'And in the back gardens. They have an arsenal of weaponry. They will take us all out, either alive or dead.'

'Capitalist running dog!' Anton rose and threw the chocolate biscuits at Jack's head. Jack shielded himself as they kept coming, biscuit after biscuit. The barrage ceased with the last of them.

'You are talking in circles, you dumb ape.'

'I don't know what you want.'

Anton, still on his feet, swung the gun along the line. 'I want to kill all of you. Except that would bring in the law and I'd have nothing to bargain with. You are my chips. I've lost one. That didn't work out too badly, but I need to play the others skilfully.' He held the gun on Jan. 'I'd so love to shoot you, sweetheart. And I am sure I will, but let it come as a complete surprise. A valentine. Something for you to live in suspense for.'

He walked along the line of them, aiming the gun at their heads one at a time. Jack thought anything could spark him. He has nothing to lose except a few hours of life. All that keeps him going is his delight in tormenting us.

'I have no illusions, Jack. I have one little pistol, they have a pile of automatic weapons all focused on me. I am not going to get out of here alive. My time is limited. Very limited. I know I can't stay awake all night, watching you. I will nod off and one of you will get this gun and shoot me. So it would be better if I shoot you all first.' He laughed, crouching low, closing one eye and aiming the pistol. 'Then the fuzz will break in and blast my head off. Finito. I'm gone. But one thing I'm resolved, I'm not spending thirty years in prison.' He squashed the empty biscuit packet, placed it carefully on the ground and let it slowly come back to size. 'My life ends here.'

'What about me?' called Susie. She was at the other end of the room in the middle of the floor, crouched on a blood-stained sleeping bag. She had not said a word for ages. Jack had almost forgotten she was there. She hardly seemed to matter in the scheme of things.

'Do what you want, Susie,' Anton called back to her. 'Leave now. I won't stop you. You're part of Red Anger. You have things to do.'

Susie rose and walked down the long room towards the others. She was dishevelled, her face streaked, dried blood streaking her jeans and T-shirt. It was as if she'd crawled out of a grave.

'Give me the gun, Anton,' she said, arm outstretched.

'Why do you want the gun?' he said.

'There's only one point to a gun,' she said with a tired smile. 'To kill someone.'

'And who might that be?'

'That would be telling. You said you liked surprises. Give me the gun, Anton.'

She was standing within a few feet of him, her hand outstretched, waiting for her gift.

'I don't trust you, Susie,' said Anton.

'Is this where you've ended up, Anton? Down the bottom of a dirty hole. Trusting no one. Waiting to die.'

'It's where I am,' he said. 'I've been heading here from every one of my foster homes. Since my dad left and my stepfather locked me in the cellar. I never expected to be loved. So why should it change at the end of my life?'

'Give me the gun, Anton.'

And she was on him, biting and snarling. He pushed her face upwards, fingers in her eyes, she kneed him in the stomach. And Jan was up, and Jack too. Susie was crying out as Anton twisted her nose. Jack grasped his wrist and smashed it over his knee. A finger poked in Jack's eye and he yelled in pain. The gun had fallen to the ground. Jan was on it – and retreated along the room.

'You snivelling ape!' she screamed, her face crawling in resentment.

Jack was rubbing his eye, half seeing in a mist of tears. He rose and stumbled towards Jan.

'Get away, Jack.' She waved him off with the gun. 'This is my fight. This cowardly creep has been threatening to kill me since we got here.'

'It's your turn, Jan,' chided Anton, stretching his arms wide to show he was a willing martyr. 'End it for me, you capitalist cow.'

He approached her, making no attempt to protect himself. Jan had both hands on the gun, arms fully outstretched.

'Shoot me, you money-stuffed pig. Exploiter of the working class.' His knees were bent in a sort of dance as he came slowly towards, chest thrust forward and welcoming.

'Hit me with your stolen wealth, fascist moll.'

A sound at the door alerted Jan and she half turned. Three men in black appeared, and in that chaotic instant - fired at her. Her body leapt in the air, arms flung in the blast. She hit the wall and slumped down to the ground.

For a lifetime, no one moved, staring at the lifeless heap, blood spitting out in tiny fountains.

Anton took a step forward. He drew the gun carefully out of Jan's hand. And, in a flash, spun round and fired at a policeman. He was bowled over in the barrage of return fire.

Chapter 37

It was five days before Jack could return to 72. It had been a crime scene for that period. As soon as the siege had come to its bloody end, he had been taken to the police station with Amina and Susie to make statements. It had taken him several hours, going through everything point by point, detailing what he saw and when. Its beginning as he ran into the house, its protracted middle, and the short ending. The police had been sympathetic, feeding him, giving him copious cups of tea, and not rushing him. But it had been an ordeal.

Jack had been on TV and interviewed by various newspapers. The day after, he'd attempted to sleep in, but the rapping on his door and the phone going non-stop made him realise it would be better to deal with the media than try to evade the news hounds.

Alison and Mia had taken him out to dinner that night. Chinese food for a change. He found speech difficult.

'Jan got shot,' said Mia as she ate her ice cream pudding. 'I saw it in Mum's paper: author of the Space Cat shot in Forest Gate siege. She was your girlfriend, wasn't she?'

'For a little while.'

'You always lose them. Don't you?'

'Mia!' exclaimed Alison. 'Your poor dad has had a terrible time.'

'Sorry, Dad. It wasn't your fault. But you're always changing girlfriends.'

Jack shrugged, keeping women wasn't his strength.

'She had a good telescope,' went on his daughter, 'I wonder what will happen to it.'

Alison rolled her eyes at her daughter's tactlessness.

She said to change the subject, 'My offer on Sebert Road has been accepted.'

'Can we go out with our telescope soon, Dad?' said Mia.

'Mia!' exclaimed Alison. 'I was telling your father about the house...'

'He's not interested,' she said. 'I can tell. But I know he likes stargazing.'

Jack gave a half laugh, but was too exhausted to engage, even with stargazing. Terror had taken its toll. He'd managed to force a little food down, but his stomach wasn't interested either. And soon after, Alison had driven him home. He didn't sleep well that night, or for the next couple of nights. And had to go to the doctor, who prescribed a sleeping pill.

It had worked. He had taken a few long walks and was definitely feeling better. Ready for work. Today, he had the key to the house that the police had given him, but was surprised to see a car in the drive and the front door of number 72 wide open.

'Hello,' he called in from the front step.

A youngish woman came out of the side room, the siege room, so to speak. She was mid 30s, in blue jeans and a chunky, blue and green sweater, with a roll neck.

'You're Jack,' she said. 'I've seen you on TV.'

'Yes, I am.' He came into the hallway. 'Who are you, if I may ask?'

'I'm Jan's sister, Dot. She told me about you. Poor Jan.' She sniffed and wiped an eye. 'Such a shock. With Mum and Dad dead,' she indicated around her, 'this is all mine now.'

'I don't understand,' exclaimed Jack. 'I thought this house belonged to Terry.'

Dot's face screwed up in puzzlement. 'Terry? Who on earth is Terry?' Then she brightened. 'Oh yes. That's Jan's middle name.'

'Are you telling me she owned this place, as well as next door?'

Dot nodded. 'Both hers.'

'It doesn't make sense,' exclaimed Jack. 'She distinctly told me she had no idea who Terry was. That the squatters were a menace.'

'She invited them in,' said Dot.

'She did what?' He was utterly perplexed.

'I don't know exactly how she did it,' said Dot. 'Through a third party, I'm sure, but she gave them the keys. And did nothing about getting rid of them.'

'I'm lost,' said Jack. 'Why on earth would anybody simply give over a house to members of Red Anger?'

'You might do that if you wanted the Choudhurys' house. Cheap.'

Jack was beginning to have an inkling.

'You mean she deliberately put in undesirables?'

'Yes,' said Dot. 'The sort no one would want to live next to. Jan was ruthless when it came to money. Very nice to family and friends, generous too. But when it came to making money, she was an out and out ruthless capitalist.'

Jack thought of what Anton had said of her, the language more foul, but much the same.

'Mr Choudhury was in debt,' said Dot. 'And Jan bought the debt, so he would have to sell.'

'Oh my God, this gets worse.'

'He'd have to sell cheap too, because who would want to live next to a band of anarchists.'

'It got her killed,' said Jack bitterly. He was leaning against the hallway wall, in need of support from the ramifications of the story he was hearing. 'You know, I was falling in love with her,' he added. 'She was lovely.'

'You didn't have a house she wanted.'

'I didn't know her at all.'

'All the easier to fall in love with,' said Dot. 'Do you want a coffee?'

'I was going to look over the house...' He stopped. 'I was

forgetting, it's yours now. Have I still got the job?'

'Of course, Jack. And there's plenty of work to do, with all the damage done in the sitting room. The plaster has been blasted to bits. It needs a total redecoration, plastering and all. Can you do that?'

'Yes, I can.'

'Make me up an estimate. I won't rush you for it. Let's go next door for a coffee.'

Dot took him to what he still thought of as Jan's house. It was warm, everything there hers. He didn't dare go into her work room.

Over coffee, Dot explained she was staying for a few days to go through Jan's things.

She said, 'I've been puzzled why the police shot Jan. It was obviously mistaken identity, but still...' She waved a hand to fill in the missing bits of thought.

'Jan had the gun after our struggle,' said Jack. 'And the police hadn't seen Anton. Didn't even have a photo of him. And Jan's hair was long, as was Anton's, she was wearing loose fitting clothes, she had her back to the cops... And then swung round on them, and they thought, in that instant, that she was Anton and about to shoot at them.'

'So they shot first,' said Dot.

Jack was filled with the image. The blasting, her flung body, the bloody and shattered flesh, the wall pitted and splashed.

'Then Anton picked up the gun,' he said. 'They thought he was one of the hostages. Until he fired at them.'

'The Kevlar jacket saved the policeman, I hear,' said Dot.

'Surface wounds,' said Jack. 'Lucky man.'

They drank their coffee in silence for a while. Jack could still see Jan sitting on the stool her sister now occupied, talking about her ideas for a new picture book, of innocent animal builders. A lifetime ago.

'What are you going to do with these houses?' he said at last.

'Well, I don't need them. And I don't want the hassle of tenants. So I'm going to sell them both. I live in Hornchurch. I've three children all settled in schools there. We live in a house we like, close to the countryside. There's no point moving here.'

'What about the Choudhurys?'

She waved both hands in exasperation. 'I'm ashamed of my sister's conduct. She had so much. Why make them homeless? These two houses, once sold, will clear me at least two and a half million. How much more do I need?'

'Sounds more than enough to me.'

'So I'm doing a deal with the Choudhurys over their debt. They can clear it over ten years.'

'Decent of you,' said Jack. He liked Dot, but then again, he'd liked Jan. Or the Jan he thought he knew.

'One should speak no ill of the dead,' said Dot, 'but Jan could be a filthy schemer. I don't have to be.'

He thanked Dot, and said he'd do the estimate today for the extra items, and get straight to work.

'It will help clear my head,' he said. 'I've the stuff outside for the patio repairs. I can get straight on with that.'

When he finished his coffee, before going round 72, Jack decided to visit the Choudhurys.

Amina opened the door for him. She beamed at once on seeing him.

'Oh, I'm so pleased to see you, Jack. Come and have tea and some of my mother's cake.'

She held the door wide for him. He came in and took his shoes off as was the custom. Today would be a slow day for sure, but some bridges had to be rebuilt. She led him into the kitchen where her mother was chopping vegetables.

'Hello, Jack,' said Mrs Choudhury. 'I hope you are fully recovered.'

'I am,' he said. 'Are you OK, Amina?'

'I'm going back to school tomorrow. But I'm fine.' She was filling the kettle for tea.

'How's Mr Choudhury?'

'Sitting up and being a complete nuisance,' said Mrs Choudhury. 'I am making some food for him. He eats the breakfast in hospital, but doesn't think much of the other food. So I am cooking every day for him.'

'He should be out in a week,' said Amina. 'Have you met Dot? She's so nice.' And then hesitated. 'Much better than her sister, I was going to say, but all considered, that's rather an unpleasant thing to say.'

'Jan was doing the dirty on you,' said Jack. 'I had no idea what she was up to.'

'Dot explained it all,' said Amina. 'And I thought Jan was so decent, arty. Nice.'

'Me too,' said Jack. 'What about the marriage plans to Wasif Khan?'

'History,' said her mother, waving a hand to erase them. 'A mistake. I should never have listened to Aklis. A stupid idea. As for locking Amina in her room... That was criminal.'

'What does your father say?' said Jack.

'He can't apologise enough,' said Amina. 'In fact, I wish he would stop. But everyone is agreed, I can go on and become a teacher. I'm looking at prospectuses now.'

'I'm pleased for you,' said Jack. 'But what brings me here, well, obviously I wanted to know how everyone was, but your patio... Do you want me to carry on with it?'

'Of course,' said Amina. 'But you must start with my window. It's just boarded up for the time being.'

'I'll do it this afternoon,' he said.

'Brilliant,' said Amina. 'Do you know what's happening to Susie?'

'The police were considering arresting her,' said Jack. 'But the case is weak. She wasn't at the bank robbery, wasn't involved in the siege – and she did help to end it. So I was told, unofficially, they won't pursue it. Chief Inspector Barker says she's gone back to her parents in Herefordshire.'

'I liked her,' said Amina. 'Even if she was rather muddled. Anton was the villain.'

'I hope she finds a better crowd,' said Jack. He rose. 'Well, I should be going. Work to do. Thank you for the tea and cake.'

'The least we can offer you, Jack,' said Mrs Choudhury. 'My husband is most apologetic to you. He said some hasty words which he regrets very much. And wonders whether you might like to bring your telescope over when he's out of hospital? With your daughter too.'

'I can think of nothing better,' said Jack.

Thank you!

I am grateful to every reader who finishes one of my novels. I have taken you on a journey which I hope you have enjoyed. There are plenty of things you could have been doing, other than reading this book. So, thank you for your time.

If you liked **Jack In The Box**, here's what you can do next:

I'd appreciate a review on Amazon. In that way, you can help me tell other readers about my books. Without reviews authors get few sales on Amazon. So I'd be grateful for your review to help this series get on the move.

You can get a **FREE** ebook of **Jack of Spades** if you sign up for my readers' list. You may give it to a friend if you wish. Every month a lucky reader from the list will be sent a **free**, signed paperback of their choice from the series. Sign up using this link:

http://eepurl.com/buAh5H

When you sign up for my readers' list you will receive my regular newsletter. This will give you news about me, what I'm reading, tell you about my future books, PLUS a variety of giveaways.

Books by DH Smith

DH Smith is the name I use for my Jack of All Trades series. The books are all standalone novels and can be read in any order.

Out Now:
- Jack of All Trades
- Jack of Spades
- Jack o'Lantern
- Jack By The Hedge
- Jack In The Box
- Jack On The Tower
- Jack Recalled
- Jack At Death's Door

Coming Soon:
- Jack At The Gate

Books by Derek Smith

All my books, other than the Jack of All Trades series, are written under the name Derek Smith.

Mystery/Crime
Murder at Any Price

Fantasy
Hell's Chimney
The Prince's Shadow
Elektra

Other
Strikers of Hanbury Street (short stories)
Catching Up (poetry)

Young Adult Novels
Hard Cash
Half a Bike
Fast Food
Frances Fairweather Demon Striker!

Children's Novels
The Good Wolf
Feather Brains
Baker's Boy

For Younger Children
The Magical World of Lucy-Anne
Lucy-Anne's Changing Ways
Jack's Bus

About the Author

I live in Forest Gate in the East End of London. In my working life, I have been a plastics chemist, a gardener and a stage manager before becoming a professional writer. I began with plays, working with several theatre companies, and had a few plays on radio and TV, as well as on the stage. In the early 80s I became involved in running a co-operative bookshop and vegetarian café in Stratford, learning to cook, and having my first go at writing a novel. The first was a mess, and, after too many rewrites, binned. The transition from drama to novels took me a couple of years to get to grips with. My first success was a young adult novel, Hard Cash, published by Faber. Buoyed up by this, I stuck with children's work, did school visits, and made a hand to mouth living as a full time author, topped up with some evening class work in creative writing at City University and the Mary Ward Centre in Holborn. A few adult fiction titles appeared from time to time, between the children's list, and I have since been working more in that direction with my Jack of All Trades series.

My full name is Derek Howard Smith. I write as DH Smith for my Jack of All Trades series; all other books appear under Derek Smith. Earlham Books is my own imprint.

www.dereksmithwriter.com

The book you're holding was designed by Lia at Free Your Words...

Contact lia@freeyourwords.com for a quote